Glory looked like an angel.

Ethan turned his gaze to the soap in the sink, then back at the solemn-looking shelter director, who'd just picked up another glass.

He wouldn't.

One corner of his lip curled up in a smile.

He couldn't.

The other corner joined the first.

He shouldn't.

Oh, but he was going to!

Ethan picked up a handful of frothy, bubbly dish soap and deposited it lightly on top of her head.

She screeched. "What did you do that for?"

He shrugged and tried to look innocent. "You look like an angel when you dry dishes, and I just thought you should have a halo."

Her green eyes sparkled with mischief. "Well, if I'm an angel...that would make you..."

She made two neat little soapsuds horns on Ethan's head.

Books by Deb Kastner

Love Inspired

DEB KASTNER

is the wife of a Reformed Episcopal minister, so it was natural for her to find her niche in the Christian/ Inspirational romance market. She enjoys tackling the issues of faith and trust within the context of a romance. Her characters range from upbeat and humorous to (her favorite) dark and brooding heroes. Her plots fall anywhere between, from a playful romp to the deeply emotional.

When she's not writing, she enjoys spending time with her husband and three girls and, whenever she can manage, attending regional dinner theater and Broadway musicals that tour her area.

A Daddy at Heart

Deb Kastner

Love Inspired

Published by Steeple Hill Books™

STEEPLE HILL BOOKS

Steeple
Hill™

ISBN 0-373-87147-3

A DADDY AT HEART

Copyright © 2001 by Debra Kastner

Visit us at www.steeplehill.com

Printed in U.S.A.

In this you greatly rejoice, though now for a little while, if need be, you have been grieved by various trials, that the genuineness of your faith, being much more precious than gold that perishes, though it is tested by fire, may be found to praise, honor and glory at the revelation of Jesus Christ.

—I Peter 1:6-7

To the LORD, for sustaining me
through the valleys as well as the mountaintops.
Without the strength, guidance and peace I've found
in my LORD Jesus Christ, there would be no light
in my days and no life in my steps.

To Joseph C., always. Without you, my books
would never see life. Bless you for coming home
from work and making dinner when I'm caught up
in my work, and for understanding that I'm not
really a space cadet—I'm just working on my book!

And to Annie, Kimmie and Katie.
Mommy loves you very much!

Chapter One

Ethan Wheeler shot a cocky grin at the woman across from him and leaned forward, resting his left forearm lightly on the cold steel of Glory Weston's desk.

Desk being a loose term, he thought as it shifted under the weight of his arm. The beat-up steel entity looked as if it had seen better days.

Lots and lots of better days, and some worse.

He pursed his lips against a smile. Most everything else in this office looked well used, from the beat-up file cabinets to the frayed white wicker trash can.

The pictures lining the walls gave the office both a professional appearance and a feminine touch, but he recognized them as prints, the type you found at a discount store. Nothing at all like the original—and very expensive—paintings he had hanging in his office.

Quite a contrast. But Ethan thrived on contrast. His confident grin widened at the thought.

The only exception to the organized chaos was shelter director Glory Weston herself. She looked as fresh as the first morning dew, her large green eyes joyfully flickering behind her glasses, and her short auburn curls bouncing with every toss of her head.

Ethan inhaled deeply of her light floral scent that had his head spinning for a moment. Nothing like the whiff of a sweet-smelling woman to start his day right, and Glory was making his day grand.

He turned his wandering attention to the stacks of paperwork lining her desk, and wondered if all the work was hers.

He thought it might be.

"Ms. Weston," he began, the first words of a well-rehearsed speech.

"Glory," she corrected, waving the file folder containing the proposal he'd given her.

The folder, he noticed with a frown, hadn't yet

been opened. His gaze swept from the file to her face, and her own gaze snared him completely.

Her eyes, even from behind aqua-colored tortoiseshell-rimmed glasses, were extraordinarily clear, making him feel as if he could read the depths of her heart, except that it was like reading a foreign language. He knew the letters but the words didn't make any sense.

What he *had* seen was a subtle shift in her emotions, a faint wariness overshadowing her politeness. He was certain his own gaze hadn't changed, so why the sudden shift in hers?

He was determined to find out. He was good at ferreting out answers to tricky questions, especially with regard to people.

"Glory." Always start with a name, especially a first name. It put things on a personal level, which was where he wanted *this* particular conversation to be. A lot rested on this discussion, but he couldn't completely put aside that he was dealing with an especially pretty woman.

The pretty woman in question pasted a smile on her face that Ethan thought was as fake as his grandmother's front teeth. She pushed her glasses up on her face with a world-weary sigh.

Civil, but just short of friendly. Fire and ice.

Even the unreliable Seattle weather didn't change that quickly.

Again, he shifted mental gears. "Look," he said, inhaling sharply. "I'm not just some guy off the street."

Glory chuckled. "Obviously."

Her gaze roved over his navy Armani suit and settled on the Serengeti sunglasses he'd half slipped into the front pocket of his crisp white cotton shirt.

Ethan fought the urge to squirm like a schoolboy. Instead, he straightened his shoulders and narrowed his gaze on her.

He didn't like the way his burgundy necktie felt suddenly, as if it were intent on strangling him, and he cleared his throat against the sensation.

"Maybe I should have sent my secretary."

She cocked a dark eyebrow over her questioning, slightly hostile eyes. "And why would that be? Not," she amended, "that I haven't dealt with my fair share of secretaries as shelter director."

Ethan shrugged, the answer suddenly eluding him. "I don't know."

He knocked a crisp beat on her desk with his knuckles and gave her his best grin. It was the best he could do at the moment.

One thing was for sure—his secretary, Mrs.

Brewster, wouldn't be so flustered and tongue-tied by Glory Weston. How was he supposed to know a knockout like Glory would be running a shelter? He'd have pulled his lawyer facade a little closer had he known, and avoided the troubles of jabbering too much or coming up blank with nothing to say.

"What's your point?"

Ow! A knockout. Literally and figuratively. The woman was nothing if not direct.

"I only meant that I thought you might be more comfortable dealing with a...woman," he ended lamely.

"Why is that?"

"The, er—subject at hand. I, uh—guess."

It was amazing how a pair of green eyes could make a lawyer who'd won national debate tournaments in college turn into a blithering idiot. He watched any semblance of maturity fly away.

"Look, Mr. Wheeler, I appreciate your concern, but I can assure you that you're no threat to me."

And I won't let you threaten my ladies, either. She didn't have to say it. He could read it in her eyes.

He wasn't a threat. She had to know. "I just thought..."

"I know," she interrupted. "And honestly, your thoughtfulness is much appreciated. However, it's quite unwarranted in this case."

She blew a wisp of hair from her forehead, and again, Ethan thought he detected a hint of weariness in her tone.

"I see."

"Do you, Mr. Wheeler?"

Ethan blinked, her candidness once again catching him off guard. "I see a perfectly capable woman who looks like she could use a vacation."

Ethan snapped his jaw closed so quickly his teeth clicked. Where had that statement come from?

"I just want to help," he muttered, furiously backpedaling.

Glory sighed and pushed up her glasses, the hint of a smile playing at the corner of her mouth. "I know you do."

She steepled her fingers and tried to examine the man before her in an impartial manner. If, indeed, the ability for her to be impartial even existed.

Even seated, Ethan Wheeler looked tall enough to balance out his broad shoulders. He was a good-looking man by anyone's standards, hers most of all.

And his smile was unquestionably contagious. When he smiled, she wanted to smile, too.

It wasn't the first time she'd been approached by a large corporation wanting to make a donation to Angel's Wings Women's Shelter, which she administrated under the authority of a local board of directors. But it was definitely the first time she'd had the CEO of such a corporation make a personal call to her downtown office where she met with clients, under this, or any other circumstances.

The *Wheeler* in Wheeler and Associates, a most respected law firm. She took a deep breath, and another good, long look. Ethan Wheeler fit the bill, but not the description.

Lawyers didn't smile, did they?

She didn't particularly care for corporate write-offs as a means of funding, since she personally thought it was more a way to knock down corporate taxes than to make a real difference to the women who sought Angel's Wings for refuge.

But beggars couldn't be choosers, no matter what her personal feelings dictated. So she'd accept the money Mr. Wheeler offered just as she'd done with many before him. Then she'd send him on his merry way, and use each dollar he gave her to the best of her ability to help the maximum number of needy women and children in her care.

She'd even gone so far as to solicit such funding, which was why, she assumed, Ethan was here.

And yet....

She met his intense, brilliant-blue-eyed gaze head-on, and he smiled crookedly in return, displaying dazzling whites she couldn't help but admire. Along with everything else about him.

The man was flawless in every feature—every hair in place, every intricate detail of his clothing attended to, from his polished leather shoes to the crisply folded burgundy paisley handkerchief peeking out of his coat pocket.

His striking gaze, and a laughing, honey-coated tenor. No doubt about it—Ethan Wheeler was one of God's finer creations. She couldn't help but admire him.

"I want to help," he said simply, reaching for the inside pocket of his suit jacket and pulling out his checkbook.

For a reason unclear to Glory, she believed him. She didn't even cringe when the leather of his checkbook cover slapped onto the desktop.

"Thank you." She cleared her throat. "I believe I can speak for the Angel's Wings' board of directors when I tell you your money is both needed and appreciated.''

His smile dipped and wavered for a moment. Pain flashed in his eyes before he dropped his gaze, suddenly intent on selecting a pen from the variety of writing utensils in the glass pickle jar on her desk.

Glory wondered at what she saw, trying to discern a personal element in this meeting, a reason beyond a simple tax write-off. Her heart suggested he cared, and she speculated on the numerous possibilities that impression aroused.

He'd grown up in an abusive home? He'd had personal contact with a battered woman? His secretary, maybe? A friend?

Then again, it might be something as dispassionate and impersonal as having seen an investigative report on a prime time television news show. Or, as she'd first suspected, a donation to offset his Learjet and his summer home on the Hawaiian Islands, only with a Do Good for Humanity tag on it.

In any case, he looked distinctly uncomfortable.

Ethan cleared his throat and tapped his checkbook on the desktop, turning it one-quarter turn for each tap. "I didn't come here to donate money.''

He straightened suddenly, crossing his arms across his broad chest. He looked up and met her gaze, which only served to confuse her more.

"At least, I don't want to contribute *just* money." Abruptly, he slapped the checkbook to the table.

She couldn't tell if he looked more annoyed or frustrated. On examination, she decided he looked both.

"Go on," she urged.

"I can give you some money, too, if you need it. But will you look at my proposal? Please?"

Her eyes widened, and she nodded. For a man who didn't want to donate money, his checkbook was certainly prominent, yet there *was* something else...something important to him. Curious, she flipped open the file and began reading.

The blue-backed papers inside looked like a business contract, and as she read the title, she discovered that it was, in fact, a legal document.

Legalese with who-knew-what meaning. Latin and politics hadn't been her forte in college. She looked at Ethan and cocked a brow.

"I'm a lawyer," he admitted wryly, pursing his lips in a way that was just short of a smirk. "Contracts are my language."

She chuckled. "Well, they aren't mine. Do you care to interpret for me?"

Ethan blinked and cleared his throat. "I want to buy computers for your shelter, have them installed on a network, and get some extra phone lines put in so the women in your shelter will have access to the Internet," he said in one breath.

"I see," she said, though she didn't.

He stood so suddenly his chair spun on its casters. Leaning forward across the desk, he rested his knuckles on the file folder and caught her gaze with his.

"Anyone can give you money," he said, his voice low and fervent. "But money often gets routed into needless or unnecessary administrative details. No fault of yours, of course," he amended with a nod and chuckle in her direction.

"Of course," she answered wryly.

"I'm not doing this very well. The point I'm trying to make is that I want to do more for you." He paused. "For Angel's Wings."

"In the form of buying computers."

"Buying and *maintaining* computers. Head to toe. Extra phone lines and everything." He grinned persuasively. "I'm ready to write you a check today to cover setup expenses."

Now that he was standing, he was nearly dancing around her desk, both in an effort to convince her and as a way to release excess energy. The man exuded energy.

"I'll be back regularly to make sure everything is carried out as planned. I won't miss a single detail, I promise." He chuckled. "Easy as pie, punch and all those other *P* words. All you have to do today is sign on the dotted line."

"Said the spider to the fly," she said, teasing the self-assured man.

Color rushed to his face, a trait Glory found endearing in a man who looked as if he'd already taken on the world and won.

An idea hovered at the edge of her mind, and Glory mentally scrambled for it. It wasn't the first time she'd experienced the still, small twinge of heart that marked time with God doing His work, whispering His will in her ears.

But what did He want her to do?

Like a spring butterfly, the answer slipped past her grasp, flaunting itself and then eluding her just as it was about to land.

Ethan crossed his arms and stood silent, watching her reaction to his plans. His gaze went from amused to worried and back a hundred times, but he didn't say a word.

The feeling of God's peace grew as she

watched the man. God had plans for Ethan Wheeler, plans that included her in some way.

But what? Glory prayed in silent petition to her Maker. *What do I have to do with Ethan Wheeler? Why is he really here?*

"I can see you need time to think it over," he said, his voice toned down a notch from where it had been before, his excitement dampened like a spring thunderstorm.

"No, it's not that," she assured, though he didn't react to her words.

"You'll want the opportunity to run it by the board of directors, of course. You can't make a decision of this magnitude on your own, right this very minute."

She opened her mouth to reply, but he appeared to have worked it out himself within his monologue.

He gave her a short smile. "I run a business. And I know how nonprofits work." He shook his head. "Sorry. Temporary brain lapse."

She nodded, stunned. God was pulling, Ethan was pushing, and she was most definitely trapped in the middle. Strained to the point of snapping, she thought wryly.

Not that it was anything new to be in the middle of a spiritual tug-of-war. God tended to spring things on her suddenly, something that went against her grain. She was stable. Organized. Self-controlled.

Maybe that was it. Maybe God was throwing Ethan Wheeler into her life to keep her off balance, to keep her reaching for the Lord and not depend on herself for everything. Reaching.

She was reaching now. She stood and came around to the front of the desk.

"When will I see you again?" she rasped, embarrassed that her voice sounded hoarse. She straightened her shoulders and regained her dignity.

He pressed a business card into her palm. "Please give me a call when you've made your decision. You can leave a message with my secretary at my office, or please feel free to call my cell phone. Oh, and I've written my home telephone number on the back."

He gave a guttural chuckle. "I know you can see I'm anxious to get started."

With crisp movements, he flipped his checkbook open and scrawled numbers and a quick signature. "Here's a thousand bucks."

"A thousand bucks?" she echoed, her voice having gone from hoarse to shrill. Hurriedly, she shifted her gaze to the file still in her hand.

His smile was wide and firm and never wavered for a second, though she couldn't say the same for his gaze, which moved from his checkbook to her and back again.

"Use the money however you want. Give it to your board for administration and paperwork and all that good stuff." He winked and grinned. "We can talk computers later, at your convenience."

His words were soft, but everything he said hit her with the force of a bullet. And every other phrase in his vocabulary was presented in a teasing tone.

After an exaggerated look at his wristwatch, he shrugged and continued.

"Mmm. Look at the time. My Meggie is waiting at home for me." He paused and winked. "You know how women can be. So I'll leave you to it. Have a great evening and don't work too hard."

The first thought to hit Glory was that he intended to leave. Of course he did. He'd pocketed his checkbook, turned around and was hiking toward the door with crisp, even steps. He didn't pause or look back.

Her second thought was of Meggie.

He was going home to a woman named Meggie. It certainly didn't surprise her that Ethan wasn't available. He was no doubt happily married with 3.2 kids and a dog.

What *did* surprise her was that she'd noticed Ethan at all—as a man. She certainly didn't notice *every* man who walked in her door. And in her experience, the old adage that all the good men were taken held true.

Of course a man like Ethan would have a woman in his life. He wasn't wearing a wedding ring, but that didn't signify anything these days.

She quickly gathered her wayward thoughts as Ethan reached the door. She couldn't let him walk away from her without giving him an answer.

And much more than that, without giving *God* an answer.

If only it were that simple.

Minor problems and quibbles aside, she didn't know the question, much less the answer she was to give.

And then, suddenly, she did know, and she wanted to laugh at how simple it really was. She refrained from laughing, but her smile was wide and steady.

"Mr. Wheeler, do you believe in God?"

Chapter Two

She hadn't realized she'd voiced her thought aloud until he'd turned an about-face on his toes, and she recognized the expression of sheer astonishment that he wore.

She looked away as a wave of dizziness made her stomach roil. One second she was in perfect peace. The next moment she was mortified, absolutely and completely mortified.

The spiritual lives of the CEOs making charitable tax deductions to Angel's Wings was less than none of her business. And to blurt out such a personal question was rude under any circumstances, most especially when speaking to a complete stranger, as she had with Ethan Wheeler.

But he'd been walking away. What else was there to do? And it had been right. Somehow, she knew it had been right.

He'd frozen in place for a moment, then slowly walked toward her, his lips pressed together in a firm, straight line. He narrowed his gaze on her, and Glory experienced an alarming feeling that he might yell at her.

She cringed inwardly that her fear instinct could still be raised so easily. Outside, she remained composed, ready for whatever passed.

He wouldn't be the first man to raise his voice, and she'd known many; both as the director of the women's shelter, and in her own life as a child with an abusive father.

For a moment, Ethan merely stood silent and watched her. She wondered if he could see the jarring emotional ride she was taking.

When he did speak, his voice was anything but loud, and Glory let out a sigh of relief. His warm tenor was soft and calm, perhaps even amused, if she didn't miss her guess. "Why do you ask?"

Now that was the question of the hour. Why *had* she asked? She wished she knew.

She glanced down at the check she still held in her hand, trying to recall what her sudden burst of genius had been all about.

She licked her dry lips and plunged in. "This check is from your personal account."

Ethan shrugged. "You don't take donations from individuals?"

"Oh, no. I mean—yes. Not usually for such high dollar amounts, but—"

"You thought I was another stone-hearted businessman looking for a tax break."

Heat rushed to her cheeks, and she harbored no hope that he'd miss her red-faced embarrassment.

To Glory, Ethan appeared to be the type of man who didn't miss much. She pushed her glasses up, then hastily dropped her arms when she realized she was calling additional attention to her flushed face.

"I really didn't think that, Ethan," she said.

It was the truth. Granted, she'd suspected his motives when he'd first walked in, sparkling like a new penny.

But now...what *did* she think?

Frowning at Glory, Ethan stroked his jaw with his thumb and forefinger. He needed a shave already, having inherited his tendency toward a five-o'clock shadow from his father.

He wished he could have had some time to think everything over, which had been his reason for attempting a hasty exit. He had a bad habit of acting and speaking first and regretting it later.

He wasn't sure why he'd come here tonight, except that he'd considered his plans and couldn't wait to get them in motion. He couldn't wait to sweep some of the guilt from his back.

On the bright side, meeting Glory had certainly been an unexpected pleasure, even if it threw him off balance. Being around pretty women always did.

This was different, though. Glory Weston wasn't like other women of his acquaintance. She'd stand out in any crowd with that red hair of hers, but there was much more to Glory than that.

He'd known plenty of women who would, given the opportunity and the motive, knock a man down and tread all over him. Who only wanted the best for themselves, and were oblivious to everything and everyone else around them.

A man could only handle a woman like that for so long before he had to make a break for it. Ethan grinned at the thought, and Glory smiled back at him, subtly shifting from one foot to the other, her only concession to the impatience he guessed she felt.

Glory wasn't like those other women. She appeared more like one of those quiet and efficient women, the ones who could run the world without raising her voice.

She wasn't that, either, though.

Glory was the better part of both kinds of women, with a little sugar mixed in for good measure.

He was woolgathering, and Glory was waiting.

But how to answer her question?

Did he believe in God?

Was this a yes or no question?

"I guess I fall into the category of slight to moderate," he said after a pause.

Honesty, however, would definitely be the best policy here. Was there some sort of spiritual requirement to donate to a Christian charity such as Angel's Wings?

He was uncomfortable revealing *any* personal information. He couldn't think of an easy way out, but didn't want to weave a web of lies.

His private life was private, though, and for good reason. He frowned.

"Sitting on a fence?" Her tone was carefully light and nonjudgmental, but curious. Ethan guessed that was for her benefit as much as his, considering the pleasant blush across her cheeks.

"Yes, I suppose I am a fence-sitter. I believe

in the God of the Bible. But I have to admit I'm a sporadic churchgoer." He cringed inwardly. "I have some...*sticky wickets* I need to work out." He broke his gaze away from hers and stared unseeingly at one of the prints on her wall.

Glory nodded. "I understand."

Ethan swung his gaze back to her. "Yeah?"

She made a choking sound in her throat. "Let's just say, 'Been there, done that.'"

Again, a pat answer, but he could see by the serious look in her eyes she was telling the truth.

"Why do you ask about my faith?" Might as well be as up-front as she was trying to be. "Is there some kind of spiritual requirements for donators or something? Do I need to sign a statement of faith?"

"No, Ethan." She waved the check like a flag of surrender. "No requirements. Listen, I'm going to hang on to this check until I've spoken to the board. Our next scheduled meeting is a week from Friday, so I should know soon."

"Great!"

"Definitely. Unless I miss my guess, the board will be unanimously ecstatic about your proposal." She smiled widely at him, but she was back to her business presentation. "And about your generous support."

He shrugged and looked away, oddly disappointed that she'd closed up as quickly as she'd flowered. "It's nothing."

Glory wanted to deny his statement, to make him see how much his generosity would help these desperate women and children who had no place else to go, no one else to turn to. He had no way of knowing the joy even a small gesture could do.

And this was grand. But she'd seen his expression on other faces at other times, and knew her words would fall on deaf ears. They would mean nothing to the man before her.

He didn't see the magnitude of his own good works. As good-natured and pleasant as he was, he was burdened, and burdened heavily.

But God changed hearts. He changed lives. And He removed burdens, taking them upon Himself.

She'd been the same way not so long ago—the expression she recognized on Ethan was reminiscent of the one she saw when she had looked in the mirror.

Still, she couldn't finish the conversation she'd started, couldn't discuss her faith. Ethan's faith.

Maybe in time....

He wouldn't believe her words, but she knew

something he would believe. "I've got some ideas of my own to run by the board, and...other inquiries to make," she said evasively.

A background check on Ethan was at the top of her list, but she couldn't tell him that—not yet, anyway. Ethan was a lawyer. Surely he knew he'd be investigated—an absolute imperative where a battered women's shelter was concerned, even for donators.

It was a frightening and sobering job, running a battered women's shelter. More than once, she'd discovered a donator to be an enraged husband attempting to get his wife back.

Ethan didn't fall into that category. She was sure of it. Still...policies had to be enforced, and procedures followed.

Ethan grinned, and she smiled back. "I'll speak with the board tomorrow morning, and then I'll be in touch."

"In touch," Ethan repeated softly, his warm voice sending a tremor of delight through Glory's veins.

And then he smiled, and her world tilted. "I'll be looking forward to that."

Chapter Three

As Glory suspected, the board voted unanimously in favor of implementing Ethan's program, including her added suggestions about the man in question.

So it was a mere two weeks later that she found herself calling Ethan's office, her heart beating erratically as she waited for his secretary to transfer the call to his office. As elevator music played in her ears, she rehearsed what she might say to him.

Nothing sounded right to her. She couldn't think of a single rational, intelligent thing to say, beyond hello.

Where was her professional polish? Where was

the facade that kept her calm, cool and collected in the varied and sometimes dangerous situations she found herself in?

She'd obviously left her refinement at home, for anxiety overrode any sense of coherent thought. She hadn't been this nervous talking to a man in years, maybe since high school.

At length, Ethan finally answered.

It was now or never, with *now* definitely pulling into the lead. She took a deep breath, ran her tongue across her dry lips and plunged in.

"Ethan, it's Glory Weston with Angel's Wings."

So far, so good.

"Glad to hear from you."

She clutched the phone closer at the pleasant sound of his rich tenor. "I hope you'll be equally glad to hear the board unanimously approved your proposal. I'd—" she cleared her throat "—*we'd* like you to come down to the shelter at your earliest convenience to tour our facilities.

"You'll also be able to examine our electrical situation and make up a preliminary list of changes we'll need to make in order to implement your program." It was only as she swept in a breath that she realized she'd been rambling.

It wasn't like her to babble. Her sister Ginger

was the talkative one of the family. Glory was the quiet one. *Usually.*

Glad he couldn't see her blush, she closed her mouth and allowed the phone line to crackle quietly.

"How does this evening sound?"

Her heart bolted to life. You'd have thought he'd asked her out or something. Too bad it was a simple business arrangement.

"Tonight would be perfect."

Trembling with eagerness, she gave him directions to the shelter. They agreed on a time, and the line went static again.

"Oh—and Ethan?"

"Hmm?"

She swallowed hard and forced the words through her lips. "Feel free to bring Meggie with you this evening."

"Really? I'm glad you offered. I like to take her with me everywhere, and I think she'd love to come along. I'll just bet you two will become fast friends."

She pressed her lips together. "I'm certain we will be."

It wasn't difficult to hear the affection and enthusiasm in Ethan's voice for the wonderful lady in his life. She wondered if Meggie knew just how blessed she was. She hoped so, for Ethan's sake.

Ethan arrived at the shelter ten minutes early, and though he'd turned off the ignition to his convertible, he made no move to enter the building.

"Guess this is it, huh, Meggie girl?"

Meggie didn't answer, but then, he hadn't expected her to. She was busily looking out the window, and obviously enraptured by what she saw.

It was a pretty view. To his surprise, the shelter was a large, well-kept blue-with-white-trim Victorian house set back in a patch of blue spruce. A white picket porch surrounded the entire house, and there was a large garden with a gazebo in the middle.

The property was marked by a white picket fence, but that was the extent of protection, as far as Ethan could see. He was no doubt missing the true security, a service perhaps, or guard dogs.

It bothered him that he could pull all the way up to the house and no one even stopped him. What if a batterer came looking for his wife?

He decided he'd have to bring the subject up with Glory. He was sure she'd have an explanation.

He tapped his palms against the steering wheel, then sat back and jammed his fingers through his hair. "I don't know why I'm nervous. I couldn't have asked for things to turn out better than they did."

That wasn't entirely true; part of his nervousness was that he was attracted to the shelter's pretty director.

And that was nothing to say about the importance of this project. He *needed* to succeed.

When he couldn't delay any longer, he made his way to the front door, glad Meggie's hand was tucked firmly in his. She gave him a sense of strength, peacefulness and composure that he wouldn't otherwise have had, just by her very presence here.

Glory met him at the door with a smile and a welcome. Immediately her gaze switched to the sweetheart on his arm, and she pushed up her glasses and exclaimed her delighted surprise.

"So this is Meggie? Come in! Come in! I can't say how pleased I am to meet you, Meggie."

Ethan glanced down at his adorable blond, curly-haired adopted daughter and smiled, his chest swelling with a father's love and pride. "Meggie, meet Miss Weston."

Meggie gave her best curtsy, and Ethan chuckled. "I think she's pleased to meet you, too."

Glory laughed as she recovered her composure. Her heart soared. Meggie was a toddler! She stooped to the child's level.

"You can call me Miss Glory. All the other children here do."

Meggie nodded, her eyes wide. "Miss Glory. You smell good."

Ethan and Glory shared their laughter as Meggie took a big whiff of Miss Glory's floral perfume. "Smell her, Papa Ethan."

Ethan's eyes lit with friendly fire. "I may just have to do that, sweetheart."

Glory didn't know whether to take his statement as a threat or a promise. His eyes suggested both. And always, there was mirth.

"Would you like to make some new friends?" she asked hastily, trying to divert attention from her perfume. "We have a lot of children just your age living here, and I'm sure they'd like to play with you. If Papa Ethan doesn't mind, you can play in our dayroom."

Meggie nodded, then held her arms up to Ethan. "Up, Papa Ethan. Up."

Papa Ethan scooped the child up with one

quick, efficient movement, and a broad grin to match. "Show us the way, Miss Glory."

As good as Ethan looked in Armani, he looked that much better in faded blue jeans and a tight white T-shirt. She definitely preferred the casual look, though he wore both styles with equal ease.

Mentally stilling her racing heart, she showed her two guests inside and began their quick tour. Their first stop was one of the two large dayrooms filled with couches, beanbags for the children, blaring televisions and a hodgepodge of long, mismatched scuffed coffee tables.

Equally mismatching square end tables in every corner were topped with brightly colored floral bouquets that gave life to the room. Even the wallpaper had flowers on it, a recent addition she was especially pleased with, considering she'd pasted the wall herself and picked out the pattern. She loved the look and smell of flowers of every variety.

Leading her visitors down the hall, she briefly passed by a few small, sparsely fitted sitting rooms with large, square windows which needed to be cleaned.

Shelter ladies used these rooms often as a haven to which they could retire when they needed to be alone.

It wasn't much, but she knew how much the women treasured their quiet time.

With a grand gesture, she introduced her favorite room in the shelter, the chapel. The room was outfitted with a crude altar, a wooden cross on the wall with a beautiful, sheer white scarf laced through it, and a couple of rough benches with kneelers for prayer.

She'd hung stained-glass pictures on the walls, one of the Good Shepherd with His sheep, and another of the Holy Spirit racing straight to heaven on the wings of a dove.

Every time she stepped into the chapel, she forgot her troubles for a moment in the solitude of peace, and experienced a renewal of strength for the great fight she fought in Jesus' name. She closed her eyes and inhaled deeply.

"Beautiful," Ethan complimented in a whisper.

Funny, how everyone always whispered in the chapel.

"Nice pictures."

Glory was jolted back to the present with his words. She smoothed her jeans with her palms. "Thanks. This room is my favorite."

"I can see why," he said, his voice low and scratchy.

He sounded uncomfortable, so she moved on

without further comment. She'd already been over that territory on their first visit.

She wanted to remind him of the joy of faith in Christ and a personal relationship with God, but first she needed to prove his trust in her was warranted. She didn't know the burdens he carried, only that he suffered, despite his naturally joyful and exuberant personality.

Reluctantly, she showed him to a large, concrete-walled dining room filled with long, foldable tables that reminded Glory of a high school cafeteria, especially with the way the echo of voices blared when the room was full.

It was a far cry from relaxing and homey, in her opinion, which was the atmosphere she constantly strove for for the ladies and children here at Angel's Wings.

With the dining room, she didn't even know where to start. Flowers, even bouquets in vases, were difficult in a room that saw so many people through it in a day, with tables folding up and down and being pushed around at the same rate.

She rushed on through, gesturing to the kitchen before moving on. At Ethan's insistence, they skipped the women's living quarters in respect to those housed there.

He was quite resolute not to cause any harm,

even unintentionally, to Angel's Wings' inhabitants, explaining quietly that he knew for these women, men were only batterers and bums.

Instead, they wandered back to the larger of the two dayrooms, where they'd mutually agreed the computers should go.

"Might any of the ladies wander in here this evening?" he queried lightly. "I wouldn't want to take anyone by surprise."

Respect for Ethan swelled in Glory's heart, usurped only by her racing thoughts. He'd hit the nail right on the head without even knowing a jot about her intentions.

That's where you come in, Ethan Wheeler.

"They all know you're going to be here," she answered, waving him off. "Most of them are okay with men, as long as it's a comfortable, non-restrictive environment."

Ethan nodded. "Great. I'd like to meet some of them. I mean, if they know I'm here, and want to come out and say hi."

God also knew Ethan was going to be here tonight, Glory thought with a grin. And He had even bigger plans for Ethan than she did.

Speaking of plans, she hadn't yet figured out how to tactfully introduce him to the ideas she had thought up. Maybe, for now, it was better simply to keep her mouth shut and let the cards fall where they would.

God was at work here, even if Ethan was unaware of His divine intervention. He'd figure it out on his own, given time. As she well knew, God could be very persistent when He was knocking on the door of somebody's heart.

She prayed it would be Ethan's heart. He needed the peace only God could give.

"What are you smiling about?" he asked softly, so close she felt the warmth of his breath on her face.

The sound of his voice and the slight, brisk scent of his cologne did funny things to her equilibrium, and she stepped backward in response. "What?"

"Just now. You got a distant look in your eyes, and then you smiled."

"Hmm," she said, waving off any significance her expression might have held with a toss of her hand. "Who knows? Just woolgathering, I assure you."

"I don't expect you have much time for that here." He sounded so sincere it neared zealousness.

"No." Her voice was husky, and she cleared

her throat. "No, I don't. Now, if you'd like to take Meggie in with the other children...."

He shook his head and handed Meggie off to Glory, who was surprised how light, if wiggly, the toddler felt in her arms.

"You take her to see the other kids, and I'll just—" he brushed his fingers through his hair and looked around the room with a meticulous eye "—have a look at these outlets."

She nodded, glad someone was being sensible, for she certainly wasn't being anything of the sort. Her rational mind had abandoned her in favor of her senses, and they were screaming in favor of Ethan, everything about him—his sight, smell, sound, touch and....

Glory Weston, you idiot! she thought to herself, giving her head a mental smack. Get a grip on yourself this instant!

Fortunately, she had an errand to run. Away from Ethan.

It took her only minutes to deposit Meggie in the children's playroom and make her way back to the dayroom, but Ethan had disappeared. The room felt empty without him, which was ridiculous, since until this evening, he'd never set foot in the room.

There was a moment of panic when she considered that he might be after one of the women, but she knew that wasn't possible. She'd had him thoroughly investigated before accepting his offer. To say nothing of that notion of rightness God continued to nudge her with.

And last but certainly not least, Ethan had been nothing but quiet and respectful around her, and when speaking of Angel's Wings. She couldn't be wrong about him.

But where was he?

She made a thorough pass around the dayroom, then walked outside and around the shelter, calling his name to no avail.

Finally, she looked in the dining room, even stooping to look under tables, thinking Ethan might be studying the electrical system of the building.

It was the sound of water that finally alerted her to Ethan's whereabouts, although her conclusion left her quite stymied; because light peeked from beneath the kitchen door, and the sound of water running was definitely coming from there.

As she approached the kitchen door, Glory realized she heard the cheerful sound of whistling. Eyebrows raised, she burst through the door.

"Ethan, what on earth are you doing in the—"

She swallowed the rest of her sentence whole

at the sight of Ethan, up to his biceps in dishwater and wearing an exceptionally frilly white apron to cover his cotton T-shirt.

The oddest thing about the picture was Glory's reaction. Where most men would have looked ridiculous, Ethan's masculinity was heightened for donning the frills.

It was the perfect paradox, and one she wanted to study in detail, she thought with a smile.

That he was perfectly comfortable, not only in the apron, but in the dishwater, came as quite another shock for Glory. "I— What are you doing?"

Ethan grinned. "What does it look like I'm doing? Dishes."

"Yes, but—"

"They have to be done, right?"

"Yes, but—"

"And I've got two arms to scrub with, right?" Two arms and a willing heart. "Yes, but—"

"It's settled, then."

Glory shook her head, bemused. She was not at all sure she and Ethan were having the same conversation. "Er...what have we settled?"

He made a big production of shaking his wet hands off and reaching for a towel. Moments later, he launched that very same towel at her head. It pegged her squarely on the jaw, and she laughed as she unwrapped it from around her neck.

"We've settled," he explained with mock patience and a catty grin, "that you're going to dry."

Chapter Four

There was one tense moment as Glory paused, and Ethan had reason to wonder if he'd made a mistake in his effort to loosen things up a little bit.

But only for a moment.

Then she pegged him back with the towel and they both laughed. "You don't leave me much choice, now, do you?"

"You're welcome to wash," he offered, gesturing to the soapy sink full of dishes.

"No, really. Please continue."

She slipped the towel from around his neck and picked up a clean dish to dry. That small movement was enough to send the light, sweet floral scent of her perfume into his nostrils and spinning through his senses.

Grinning, he began to whistle. How long had it been since he'd done dishes?

He thought it could have been since he'd been a teenager. His older brother Erik had become stricter than his father when their mother passed away.

Not that he could strictly blame Erik. Their father had become a virtual recluse, sleeping out on the range more often than home at the ranch. Baby brother Rhett had still been a little guy, so Ethan caught the brunt of Erik's attempts to maintain civility.

Ethan had done enough dishes and housework to last a lifetime, and had sworn he'd never do such menial work again.

And he hadn't, until today, when he'd walked into the kitchen and seen the mess.

He still didn't know why he'd filled the sink with soap and tackled the disarray of plates, cups and saucers, but something inside his chest urged him on persistently.

He slid a glance to Glory, who was nibbling on her thick bottom lip, looking as if she were concentrating furiously on the glass in her hand she was shining. She looked like an overzealous bartender.

Ethan's grin froze.

She looked like an angel.

He turned his gaze to the soap in the sink, then back at the solemn-looking shelter director, who'd just picked up another glass.

He wouldn't.

One corner of his lip curled up in a smile.

He couldn't.

The other corner joined the first.

He shouldn't.

Oh, but he was going to!

Making a circle with his hands, Ethan picked up a handful of the frothy, bubbly dish soap and deposited it lightly on the top of her head.

She screeched, waving him away wildly with her hands.

"What did you do that for?" She sounded surprised, but thankfully, not angry.

He shrugged and tried to look innocent. "You know, you look like an angel when you dry dishes, and I just thought you should have a halo."

"A halo, is it?" Her green eyes sparkled with mischief. "Well, if I'm an angel—" she paused, reaching for her own handful of dish soap "—that would make you..."

She left her sentence dangling as she made two neat little soapsuds horns on Ethan's head. She had to reach on tiptoe to do it, which brought her scent and warmth dangerously near.

Ethan reached for the counter to keep from reaching for her.

"You know you're in dangerous territory now," he threatened, cocking one eyebrow.

She only smiled. "Is that so?" In two steps she was at a rinsing hose, and it only took a couple of seconds more before Ethan was the target of a long spray of cold water.

He hollered and twirled around to keep from being soaked, though all the dancing in the world wouldn't have kept him out of the cold water. But no one had ever accused him of running away from a fight.

"All's fair..." he warned with a chuckle, reaching for a glass and filling it with hot, soapy water.

She shrieked as he advanced. "At least mine's warm," he accused. He took his time, stalking her slowly, intent on his prey.

She squeaked like a mouse and tried to duck

down, but he still managed to douse her shoulder. "So it's war, is it?"

"Glory, are you okay? Glory? I heard yelling and I..."

Ethan and Glory both whirled at the sound of the voice, but Glory regained her composure first.

"Lena. I'm sorry we disturbed you." She dabbed ineffectively at her wet shoulder with the towel. "I—we—"

Ethan looked from woman to woman, wondering who looked more surprised.

Lena, whom he gathered to be a current tenant of Angel's Wings, looked mildly stunned, though he thought he saw a sparkle of understanding in her eyes.

Glory looked downright traumatized, as if they'd been caught in a misdeed.

He didn't think a water fight was too terrible an offense, and he was pretty sure Lena didn't think so, either. Still, he stepped forward cautiously, using his fingers as a comb on his dripping hair as he cleared his throat. "My name is Ethan Wheeler."

He met Lena's gaze with what he hoped was calm reassurance, though his heart continued to beat double time.

Glancing at Glory, he continued. "I'll be installing computers here at the shelter."

Lena's large brown eyes widened noticeably.

"I know," he said with a shrug. "I look like the janitor."

That brought a chuckle from both women, and his smile widened. Maybe this wouldn't be as hard as he thought.

"Glory was just showing me around."

"You're installing our computers in the kitchen?" Lena queried with a wavering smile.

It was Ethan's turn to laugh. "I'm afraid I can't take the blame here. Glory made the mistake of leaving me alone, and I got into mischief."

He slid a glance at Glory, who hadn't spoken since Lena had first entered the room. She was chewing her bottom lip again, looking as if she were trying to remember the answer to something important.

"It really is all her fault," he said, winking at both women.

"It is not!"

Glory found her voice with difficulty. She'd been mortified when Lena had found her clowning around with Ethan in the kitchen. It felt terribly, horribly wrong, having fun when the women and children just down the hall were suffering through some of the worst times of their lives.

She knew what her sister Ginger would say: Lighten up, Glory.

But she couldn't do that. It never worked for her. She was an all-or-nothing woman, and she'd just compromised her principles.

"I apologize for what it looked like," she said, firming her resolve with every word. It had been a mistake bringing Ethan here. What must poor Lena think? If she told the other women....

"It didn't look like anything." Lena turned her gaze to Glory. "How did you get a handsome guy like this to wash dishes for you? Wherever you got him from, you need to share the wealth."

A wave of sadness washed over Lena's expression, but her smile quickly returned.

Glory didn't know whether to be shocked or relieved. Glancing between Lena and Ethan, it looked like they were sharing a private joke. She seemed to be the only one making a big deal over the situation.

"Are you going to be teaching the computer classes, too, Ethan? Or is your only specialty dishes?" Lena winked at Ethan and leaned against a counter, folding her arms around her.

Ethan laughed loudly, slapped a dry towel across one shoulder, and returned to the sink.

Glory watched Lena closely, feeling she'd done Ethan a disservice. She'd given a lot of thought before introducing him to Angel's Wings, not to mention feeling it was what God wanted her to do, yet she'd completely panicked at the first real test.

Ethan *would* be good for the women at Angel's Wings. He'd easily adapted to a situation that would have sent most men fleeing for their lives.

He'd not only responded well to a withdrawn woman with a bad history where men were concerned, but he now had her comfortably conversing with him. He was certainly gifted with people.

And he was utterly charming.

"Unfortunately," he was saying, "I'm neither an expert at computers *nor* dishes."

"Which is really too bad, don't you think, Lena?" Glory teased, inching her way back into the conversation. "And to think he could have majored in soapsuds."

"A real shame," Lena agreed.

"I guess I was also laboring under the false perception that you were going to teach the computer stuff, Ethan," Glory said, bewildered. "I mean, we never really discussed it, but I just thought...."

Her sentence trailed off, but when Ethan raised his eyebrows at her, she felt it was necessary to defend herself.

"It *was* your idea."

Ethan shrugged. "It's my *money*. I'm afraid I'm not much good past the green. However, I'm certain I can locate someone appropriate for you with a little research."

"That won't be necessary," Lena said quietly. Glory and Ethan both turned to her.

"It won't?" Glory tried not to sound as befuddled as she felt.

"Of course not." She was speaking to Glory, but she never took her eyes off Ethan. "Glory's sister Ginger works in the computer industry. She'd be perfect for the job."

"Does she live in Seattle?" Ethan queried, sounding relieved to be let off the hook.

"Bothell," Glory answered quickly. "Across the lake. But I'm really not sure she's the woman for the job."

"She hangs around here enough." Lena smoothed down her hair with her palm. "She's such a friendly soul. I can't imagine that she'd mind sharing a little bit of her wisdom with us."

"Probably not," Glory admitted.

Quite the opposite, in fact, she thought, trying to bottle up her resentfulness. Ginger would no doubt steal the show, and be glad to do it.

The truth was that her sister would use this computer thing as an excuse to be around the shelter even more often than she already was. And that meant, among other things, the inevitable lectures on how big sister Glory ought to get a life.

She had a life, thank you very much, though Ginger refused to concede to the point. Still, she supposed it wasn't such a bad idea to ask her sister to help. She did know computers.

"I'll ask her," she said at last, clearing her throat against the grainy sound her voice made.

She turned to Ethan. "Does that mean you won't be here for the installation, either? I had rather thought you'd want to be here."

She didn't want to think about the reason her gut clenched at the mere thought of Ethan walking out the door tonight and never coming back.

He chuckled loudly. "You couldn't scare me away with enough bears to fill a circus," he promised. "In fact, if your sister is any good, I may just show up for the computer classes."

He winked at both of them. "That all right with

you, Lena?'' he asked, before turning to wash a plate, whistling softly.

"Oh, it's just *fine* with me.''

Lena's gaze met Glory's as she answered, her sometimes frightened brown eyes now sparkling with mirth, and Glory felt her face warm even before the next words were uttered.

"I'm sure *Glory* would *love* to have you.''

Chapter Five

Ethan leaned over the side of the white Jenny Lind crib, softly stroking Meggie's golden hair away from her forehead. She slept the sleep of the innocent, her little chest moving up and down in a slow, regular rhythm that comforted him.

Poor Meggie. She'd never know her real mother, or *any* mother, in all likelihood.

He frowned at the direction of his thoughts. He had enough to worry about without reliving events he couldn't change and pondering a future he couldn't see.

Tonight, when he'd met Lena's gaze, he'd felt such a resurgence of helplessness—of hopelessness—that he'd barely been able to contain his rage.

How could a man batter a woman—harm her
so terribly that she needed to run away from home
to escape him? Especially a husband who'd promised before God and witnesses to love and cherish
his wife? Who would be there to protect her if
the man she loved turned against her?

It was completely beyond his comprehension.

He'd asked himself that same question over and
over again in the two years since his cousin Sabrina died at the hands of her husband.

He still didn't understand. He still couldn't
comprehend such madness, such vice.

Frustration and rage poured through him. He
tempered it only by scooping the tiny form of his
still-sleeping little girl into his arms and sitting
down in the rocking chair in the corner.

Each day, more and more, she reminded him
of Sabrina. Her soft, golden hair, her sweet, innocent blue eyes. She'd be a knockout when she
was older.

Just like Sabrina.

How could God allow such things to happen?

He could still see Sabrina's face as she confided
her plans for escape, to get herself and Meggie
far away from her husband, Jason.

She'd been terrified, and it was no wonder. Jason had threatened more than once to kill her.

Sabrina had said she'd rather he hit her, because at least then she knew he wasn't going to hit Meggie.

And later, always later, Jason would brush off his threats and his abuse as no more than his Irish temper. He'd be soft and persuasive, but Sabrina had learned the hard way that it meant nothing.

Ethan still remembered the expression on her face as she sat across the booth from him in the secluded coffeehouse across from the college campus where they'd both taken prelaw, her eyes were full of determination and purpose.

Her six-month-old baby Meggie would never suffer hurt from her father, not as long as Sabrina was around to protect her.

Ethan squeezed his eyes shut against the tears forming. Sometimes he could think about Sabrina and remember the good times, smile at the happy memories, but on this cold, dark night, what he remembered was the pain.

He kissed Meggie's forehead, just where a stray curl had fallen, and for the hundredth time since he'd walked into Glory Weston's office, he wondered if he was making a mistake getting involved.

For one thing, he feared for Meggie's safety at Angel's Wings.

Meggie's father was behind bars, for the time being, anyway, but he knew the women at the shelter were hiding from men who *weren't* behind bars. And he still hadn't seen any security measures at the house.

The last thing Ethan wanted to do was let Meggie get hurt—the very reason he kept her beside him twenty-four hours a day, even to the point of opening a daycare center right next door to his law office.

He wouldn't leave Meggie behind with a babysitter. But could he abandon Glory—his project at Angel's Wings?

He *could,* of course.

The money had passed hands. The computers would be installed within a week. And Glory's sister Ginger would give the women the knowledge they needed to access the Internet and change their lives for the better.

What more was there left for him to do? That was the way he'd meant it to be, funding a project for the shelter and walking away.

He'd never meant to get involved.

But he *was* involved. Glory had seen to that. She'd trusted him enough to bring him to the shelter.

He knew deep in his heart he couldn't let Glory

down. He couldn't let Meggie down. Maybe this time around, he wouldn't let *himself* down.

After one last snuggle, he stood and placed Meggie back in her crib. He loved the smell of her—most of the time, anyway, he thought with a chuckle.

Admittedly, it would be hard for him to spend time at the shelter, to face his demons head-on. But it hadn't been as hard as he'd supposed it would be. He'd enjoyed talking to Lena, after he relaxed, and she realized he wouldn't break any unspoken boundaries between them.

Might he not be able to do the same for other women at the shelter? Be an honorable male role model for the kids, and a man these women could trust?

He frowned and shook his head at the thought. He wasn't up for sainthood. He'd already let one woman down. But at least he could wash dishes and mop floors and do any other chores that needed doing.

He brushed Meggie's curly hair back from her forehead. She brought a soft smile to his lips. Meggie was the one good thing to come from an otherwise tragic situation.

His younger brother Rhett would say God was

in control, and for the first time in many years, Ethan thought he might be right.

Maybe, just maybe, God *was* in control.

In a little over a week, the new computers were delivered and installed, and the following Saturday marked the first day of computer class. Whatever Ethan had done to hasten the process had certainly worked without a glitch.

Glory, however, had to tussle with the phone company when it came to putting in extra lines, but it was worth the trouble to see the enthusiasm in the ladies', not to mention the children's, faces.

Ethan had been right about the computers. And Lena had been right about Ginger. It had taken less than five minutes to get her younger sister to commit to an indefinite and ongoing number of weeks training the shelter women on Internet tactics for education, relocation, and eventually, employment.

She frowned down at her beat-up, legal-size brown clipboard, which she held snug to her waist with her left hand, and thoughtfully tapped a pencil against with her right.

Ostensibly, she was making notes on the first day's work in progress, but something else was bothering her far more than the overwhelming success she knew this day would be.

Ethan had promised he'd be here for the inaugural class, but there was no sign of him and Meggie. With only ten minutes to go, she was beginning to think he wouldn't show at all.

"What are you frowning about?" Ginger tapped against the back of Glory's clipboard with her fingers, sending it out of her grasp and flapping awkwardly to the ground, papers everywhere.

"Ginger," Glory protested, the note of warning in her voice so clear even her tenaciously thickheaded sister couldn't mistake it for anything else.

"You don't need that old clipboard anyway. You're too pretty to hide behind papers."

"Ginger." The protest in her eyes became a silent plea. "We're not teenagers anymore. I don't have to dress up or look pretty to run this shelter right. After all, I'm not going out on a date."

"Maybe that's just what you need," she suggested audaciously.

"What does Glory need?"

Glory whirled at the honey-rich male voice speaking just over her shoulder, and found Ethan grinning down on her, Meggie riding on his shoulders with a happy smile of her own.

"Ethan. I wasn't sure you were going to show."

Ethan raised his brows. "What? And miss the grand opening? I wouldn't think of it."

"Hello, Ethan," Ginger said, her voice annoyingly sultry as she raised her hand to shake his. "I don't think we've met."

Glory stopped just short of rolling her eyes, but she had to bite her bottom lip to keep from laughing. Her sister was terminally incorrigible in every area of her life, most especially in regard to men.

Ethan shook Ginger's hand, but his mischievous gaze was on Glory. "This must be the sister you were talking about."

"Oh, so she's mentioned me to you," Ginger gushed. "She certainly kept *you* a secret." She slid a glance at Glory, who sighed loudly.

Ethan chuckled, and Glory reached for the clipboard on the floor to hide her flushed cheeks. Fortunately for Ginger, she was in good humor, now that Ethan was here.

Her sister was doing it again. In younger years, Glory would have clocked her for such behavior.

"Are you sure you weren't switched at birth with some kid under a cabbage leaf? We can't possibly be related by blood,'' she commented wryly, pulling the clipboard under her chin. Naturally outgoing and flamboyant, Ginger was the near opposite of dedicated and determined Glory.

Staid and stodgy, Ginger would say.

For the first time, Glory worried that her sister might be right. She was mortified at the jealousy sparking through her when Ethan shook Ginger's hand, and found herself almost wishing she *did* know how to flirt with a man.

This was new ground for her. She didn't like feeling out of control, and she'd never felt so helpless as she was at that moment.

And then Ethan turned his toothy grin on her, and she completely forgot to be jealous. In fact, she forgot to breathe. It was a good thing her heart beat on its own, or she'd be in real trouble.

He swept Meggie down with a whoop, then whirled her around until she squealed with laughter. "I come bearing gifts," he said straightening, yet still holding the toddler by the hand.

"Don't you think you've done enough?" Glory asked, only now beginning to regain her equilibrium.

"I've barely started."

She wondered if that was a threat or a promise,

and hoped Ginger wouldn't ask, which of course she would.

"How so?" Glory asked unwillingly.

"I've brought two of the seven deadly sins to share with everybody." He paused dramatically and waggled his eyebrows. "Caffeine and chocolate. They're in the trunk of my car. If you can watch Meggie for a moment, I'll bring them in."

It was only a minute before Ethan returned, laden with a case of soda cans and several boxes of brownies.

He set them before her with a flourish. "I'd say I baked them myself, but you'd know I was lying. Besides, I'd rather be spending quality time at my local women's shelter."

"Is that what it's called now?" quipped Ginger, with a sly glance at her sister. "Quality time."

Ethan looked offended. "I'll have you know I'm a man of the millennium, P.C. in every way." He pursed his lips and grinned. "Perfectly Clever."

"Oh, you're that," Ginger said, laughing. "That and a *lot* more."

Glory shot her sister another warning look, wondering if her face was going to freeze that way from overuse.

"Looks like we're going to have some trouble," Ethan commented, gesturing at the neat lines of computers.

Glory spun around and ran her gaze over the area. "How's that?"

Ginger laughed. "I think he means the kids." She sashayed over to Glory and bent toward her ear. "Lighten up, sis. This is going to be fun."

Fun.

Now there was a word not in Glory Weston's dictionary. When was the last time she'd had fun?

But life wasn't about fun. It wasn't about flirting and laughing and playing, as much as Ginger might think it was.

Real life was about fighting. It was about trying to survive.

Meggie squealed as Ethan swung her to the ground. "Can you show me where the kids' dayroom is?" Ethan shrugged, making his sea-blue sweater tighten over his shoulders in a very eye-catching way.

Ginger immediately stepped forward and offered her hand to the toddler. "I'm not on for another ten minutes yet. I'd be happy to take her, and you two can talk. About whatever."

Glory opened her mouth to protest and then snapped it closed again. There was no use arguing with her sister over anything. It would just call attention to her words, and embarrass Glory further.

Ginger was hopelessly flighty, just as Glory was hopelessly grounded. God had certainly created polar opposites in her family.

Ethan reached for her hand and led her around the room, moving from computer to computer and speaking to each young occupant in turn. He made the funny video game sounds boys made and twisted and twirled his way down the aisle.

During all this, he never once let go of her hand. He'd twist it around his waist, and one time even twirled her around. She didn't know whether she felt uncomfortable because she was, in effect, dancing with the man in the middle of a crowded room with no music playing, or if it was the very touch of his hand, the crook of his mouth or the smile in his eyes that made her feel flushed.

"That's a pretty cool video game," he said to one eight-year-old boy, and ruffled his thick black hair when the boy laughed.

"This is Stephen," Glory said quietly. "He's Lena's boy."

She didn't miss the shade of pain that passed over Ethan's eyes as he took her arm and led her a short distance away. But then, with a quirk of his lips, the pain was gone, replaced by his usual good cheer.

"How long have they been here?" he asked quietly. "Lena and Stephen, I mean."

"They've been here four months. Stephen is amazingly well-adjusted to this place." She looked away. "Not every child, or woman, for that matter, does so well as the Bostwick family has done. Stephen has lived through enough anguish to last a lifetime."

Without warning, Ethan cupped her chin in his hand, gently stroking her cheek with his thumb as he turned her face to his. His breath was warm, the brisk scent of his aftershave comforting.

Glory could neither breathe nor speak, so she simply stared up at him, noting the sadness that crossed his eyes, and wishing her words hadn't put it there.

Her world was a world of pain and sorrow, and she suddenly wished she hadn't inflicted it upon smiling, good-natured Ethan. But it was too late to urge him and his child to leave and not return.

"Don't be sad, sweet Glory," he whispered softly, then dropped his hand and turned away.

She didn't want him to leave. She'd known it before, but as she'd gazed up into his shining blue eyes, feeling the tender, gentle roughness of his hand on her cheek, she thought her heart might not withstand the impact of his leaving should he go away.

Chapter Six

~⚬~

Ethan watched the swirl of women around him, most of them tired and ragged, some giving sly, interested glances in the direction of the computers; but only a couple of them actually sat down behind a computer screen.

He could fix this problem. All he needed was…a chair and a…drum.

But a brownie pan would do.

He stood on the chair and banged the aluminum pan with his fist. It wasn't pretty, but it got the job done.

"Let's get this show on the road," he announced, making the sentence sound like a song. "C'mon, Ginger, we've got some ladies here who are rea-dy."

That got him a chuckle or two. He grinned at Glory, briefly wishing he could get her to smile more. She had such a beautiful smile.

"And let's start our lesson with a hearty round of applause for the lady that made all this possible, our fantastic director, Glory Weston!"

He hopped down as the women cheered and hooted along with him. The more noise the better, as far as Ethan was concerned.

"Ethan," Glory whispered, her voice low and scratchy. "All this is your doing, not mine."

Ethan just grinned. "You just don't give yourself enough credit." He cocked an eyebrow. "Therein lies the problem, my dear," he said, hoping he sounded like an antiquated doctor.

"I'm glad you told her that," Ginger interjected. "She won't listen to me."

He hoped she'd listened to him, but like Ginger, he doubted it.

It wasn't so much that Glory had a bad self-image, as much that she was so wrapped up in what she was doing here at the center, she forgot herself completely. He'd bank on the idea of Glory having missed meals and sleep. He'd bet a dollar she spent late nights with paperwork and shelter issues, a candy bar her only meal.

Glory switched into her shelter director mode, squaring her shoulders and stepping forward.

"All of you ladies already know my sister Ginger, but I'm proud to introduce her as the new instructor for our computer and Internet classes."

After slight applause, the women settled down to work behind their computers. Some still looked stiff and uncomfortable, to Ethan's way of thinking, but he'd done the best he could, short of starting a conga line.

Not such a bad idea at that, except Glory would throw him out on his can. And for some reason, he didn't want to be thrown out, at least not yet. Not until he'd been able to corner the irascible shelter director someplace private.

It was half his reason for coming. He'd made a promise to Meggie, and he was going to keep it. With a secretive smile, he winked at Ginger and swept through the aisle, helping out whenever he could, if the lady in question was open to help from a man.

Some weren't, and that was okay. He made a mental note of their names and faces and gave them the room they needed, knowing they wouldn't appreciate his antics, and knowing they had every right to feel that way.

He only hoped he could let them know, in

whatever way possible, that not all men were lying, cheating, abusive nozzles.

That some men were honest, respectful and most of all, trustworthy.

Glory was doing her own mulling as she perused the room, worried not so much about the ladies' reaction to Ethan as their reaction to the computers. Most of them hadn't finished high school, much less become acquainted with a computer. She was certain some of these women were climbing mountains just to be sitting before an electronic device.

But she knew they'd do anything, no matter how difficult, that would help them pull themselves up, find new lives to live. Beat down by life as they were, they were some of the strongest women she'd ever met.

Glory liked to hope they'd find excitement in what was ahead, once they became familiar with the Internet and the freedom it offered them.

They could get a degree, find a house, get a job. A new relationship was the last thing they wanted now, of course, but Glory hoped it for them, someday.

Her glance rose to Ethan. He planned to financially sponsor any woman who wanted to pursue their degree, whether a high school diploma or beyond.

The man was nothing short of amazing. He drove her crazy with his silly antics, but he did things for others Glory could only begin to conceive of. And he did it all with that sly pucker on his face that labeled him an irascible urchin.

"Just push the backward arrow there, Susan," she said, leaning over one of the women. "You pushed the forward arrow one too many times."

"This mouse is kind of tricky," Susan commented, wiggling the item in question.

Glory chuckled. "That it is. I wonder why it's called a mouse?"

"The tail," said a male voice from behind her. Ethan leaned over her and picked up the mouse, demonstrating.

By this time he had everyone's attention, of course, and Glory thought he probably knew it. He was a natural extrovert.

He pulled a black marker from his back jeans pocket. Glory watched in astonishment as he drew eyes, a nose, and whiskers on the item. A mouse!

Then, with a grin, he wiggled it again, allowing the cord to flop around.

"See? A mouse."

"It really does look like an animal, once you

put life into it, Ethan," Susan said, laughing heartily. "But now, how am I going to work this ridiculous computer?"

She paused for effect. "I'm absolutely terrified of rodents."

Glory burst out laughing. "A hedgehog, maybe? How about a Chihuahua?" she suggested mildly.

"Nah," Ethan disagreed with a grunt. "Who'd want to drag around a Chihuahua all day?"

Taking the pen in hand again, he drew two pointed ears. "Kitten. A nice, soft, sweet, cuddly kitten." He placed the mouse back down on the mouse pad and lifted his pen. "Anyone else?"

Nearly every woman wanted Ethan to change her mouse into a kitten, or at least an animated mouse, and he was happy to oblige.

With his mouth in that cute little smirk it made, he moved from computer to computer, making every woman feel like the only person in the room.

Ethan had a way about him. He could do more for these women in a minute than she could do with weeks of work. She sent up a silent, thankful prayer that God had brought Ethan into her life, and ignored the plunge of the poisonous dagger of jealousy.

She did what she could…but she could *not* do what Ethan did.

"How far are we going today?" she asked Ginger, who was regarding her with decided interest. She ignored the look, though her hackles rose.

"I just wanted to show them how to get online, and then let them play a little bit. Next week I'll start getting into specifics on education, housing and employment." She paused and pushed a bushy wave of blond hair out of her eyes. "Was there anything else you wanted me to cover today?"

Glory shook her head. "You're definitely the expert in this field."

"Not expert enough," Ginger replied, sliding a glance at Ethan.

"What's that supposed to mean?"

"Nothing. I just think maybe you need to get out once in a while."

"Ginger, we've been over this ground before. God has given me this work to do, and I don't have time to date."

She just smiled. "But you want to marry."

"God is able to provide," Glory stated, wishing she didn't sound defensive but knowing that she was.

"Oh, He's able to provide, all right," Ginger

said with a wry laugh. "If Glory won't move to the man, God will have to move the man to Glory."

She swatted Ginger affectionately on the sleeve. "You are, always have been, and always will be, incorrigible. Give or take a few minutes at birth, when you were just cute."

The sisters laughed comfortably. They might be opposites in every way, but there was only love between them. Their difficult background had allowed—no, forced—them to cling together more than other sisters, and in a cockeyed kind of way, Glory was glad.

Ginger had been looking off in the distance—probably thinking the same things Glory was. But suddenly she turned her head back, and the happy light was back in her eyes.

"I've got to have some duct tape," she announced, as if this were an everyday request.

"Duct tape?"

"Yeah. Uh—duct tape. From the uh—supply room. I'm sure I saw some up there on the shelves. You wouldn't mind getting it for me, would you, sis?"

"And you need duct tape for...?"

Ginger glanced around furtively. "Uh...."

It was beginning to be Ginger's favorite phrase, and Glory smelled a trap.

Suddenly Ginger smiled and turned her around by the shoulders with a short push off toward the supply room.

"Duct tape. To tape down all the computer wires so the kids don't trip on them. I need it right away. But I can't leave. Please?"

That sounded reasonable, though Glory did wonder why Ginger—and Ethan, and the computer techs who'd originally set up the systems— had failed to have taped the wires down in the first place.

Glory shook her head and headed for the supply room. Perhaps it was just an oversight. This had all happened so fast.

It was a big job, and she was glad Ginger had noticed the cords. There was so much that could go wrong, and they'd been blessed to have been so free of problems.

She was certain the teenagers here at the shelter would be all over the computers every chance they got, and since teens—especially boys— didn't move at a speed less than Mach 3, taping down the lines wasn't just a good idea, it was a necessity.

She was just reaching for the tape on an upper

shelf, hoping she wouldn't tip the entire steel-beamed shelving unit over on top of her, when the lights went out. Not even a flicker of warning, and she was in pitch black.

For a moment she couldn't see at all, until her eyes recovered from the unexpected surprise. The darkness didn't bother her, since she'd left the door propped slightly open when she'd come in.

She was, however, standing motionless in the half-dark thinking about what an electrical shortage might have done to the computers. She prayed they were still working. If, after all the work everyone had done, they lost the computers to a power failure, she didn't know what she'd do.

A moment later the door slammed with a resounding crack, leaving her in total darkness. Her heart pumped wildly against her throat with the sudden noise, but it wasn't until she moved to open the thick wood door and found it locked, did she really panic.

She pounded as hard as she could and yelled for all she was worth.

"Ethan! Ginger! Anybody! *H-e-l-p!*"

Chapter Seven

A match ticked against a box, and the small, steady glow of a miniature candle, the kind she'd put on a birthday cake, flickered against the darkness.

"No need to shout," came a tenor voice from behind the flicker. "Help is on its way."

"Ethan!" She didn't know whether she was more irritated or relieved.

He stepped forward, so she could see his high, crooked grin against the glow of the candle, which she could now see was placed in the middle of a Twinkie.

"You'd better blow it out before wax drips on the creamy middle. It's my favorite part."

She lifted an eyebrow, but doubted Ethan could see it. Still, she didn't speak.

Neither did he, for a moment, so she did the unimaginable. The unconceivable. At least for Glory Weston, it was.

She blew out the candle.

The top lights flicked on as quickly as they had gone out, temporarily blinding Glory. She held a hand up to her eyes.

"Happy, happy, happy, happy, happy anniversary," Ethan sang, twirling around her with his Twinkie.

With a flourish, he took a big dip of cream on his forefinger and brushed it across her lips.

"Happy *what?*" she asked around her mouthful of cream.

"Anniversary. Happy *anniversary.* I'm wounded you didn't remember."

"I'm sorry. I didn't mean to—" She stopped herself flat, suspicion arising as fast as her gaze was narrowing.

"*Whose* anniversary are we celebrating?" she asked, her voice an octave higher and a good deal more screechy than she would have liked.

"Ours, of course."

Now who would have known?

She should have, in a way, at least. He looked

like a little boy. A bright, happy little boy ready
to celebrate in earnest. "I wanted to make it a
cupcake, but your vending machine only had
Twinkies."

Cupcakes. Twinkies. Anniversaries. Glory was
stunned and bewildered, and she knew it showed
on her face. She hadn't had this much variety in
her life since her teen years, and maybe not even
then.

Ethan felt like a military jet against her motor-
less glider.

"Today," he said, leaning close to her face, "is
the one-month anniversary of the day we met."

Glory tried not to notice the cream on the corner of his mouth, tried to look in any direction
but at Ethan, which was a challenge with him so
near, invading her space.

"That's nice," she said at last, feeling as if he
were waiting for her to speak.

"Nice? You haven't *had* nice, yet. Meggie and
I have some special plans for next weekend, and
you're invited."

It wasn't exactly a question, so Glory, as usual,
didn't know how to respond.

Actually, she did; she just was afraid to say the
words.

"Ethan, I can't be away from the shelter on the

weekend. It's my busiest time, as you can see from today. The women need me.''

Ethan reached for her hands, and just stood quietly before her for a moment, looking down at her with his warm, twinkling gaze, and softly brushing her palms with his thumbs.

"They'll get along without you for one Saturday."

"Ethan, I—"

"Ginger said you'd give me grief on this. Don't you want to prove your sister wrong?"

"What's Ginger got to do with this?"

"*Ginger's* going to cover for you," he said softly, persuasively.

He dropped her hands and cupped her chin, tipping her head up to meet his eyes. "She'll be here anyway, teaching computer lessons. She knows what to do, Glory. And she can handle it."

"I know, but—"

"I talked to a few of the women in the shelter. They're okay with this. More than okay. They're rooting for you.

"Glory, you need to get outside. Enjoy the scenery. See God's grandeur. Live it up a little bit."

He slid his hands down her neck to her shoulders, and she stopped breathing. "Come with me to Puget Sound. Smell the sea, embrace the air.''

''Ethan, God's called me to—''

''God didn't call you to live apart from the world, Glory. *In* the world, but not out of it.''

He pulled her closer, pleading as much with the gentle caresses of his hands as he was with the tone of his voice, more serious than she'd ever heard him.

''Glory, please. Come with us.''

The silent air between them thickened and Glory swallowed hard.

What could she say?

What was the right answer to Ethan's simple question?

What would God want her to do?

She'd never been faced with such a situation, and it floored her physically, emotionally and spiritually.

For a moment, she wished him away. Without Ethan in the picture, her way was clear and un-cluttered.

Yet Ethan brought so much warmth and light with him wherever he went. He encouraged the work of God, with his money, but much more with his presence.

And yet....

Abruptly Ethan turned and stepped away. "Well...."

He said the word as a goodbye. Glory pinched her eyes closed against the tide of emotions running through her.

"Well...." she repeated.

Ethan looked back for a brief moment, then puckered his lips in that way he had, and walked out of the storage room. Cocky, confident and whistling softly under his breath.

The man defied incorrigible. He was irritating, annoying, sometimes obnoxious and absolutely endearing. How would she ever get by?

Whistling a bouncy polka, Ethan adjusted his tie and gazed at the figure he made in his full-length mirror. Dark denim jeans, a crisp white linen shirt, and a paisley tie that felt a little too tight.

Meggie tottered into the room, and he immediately crouched down to her level. She reached for his tie and gave it a strong tug.

"Lose the tie, huh?" he asked, chuckling when she answered him in baby talk. "I thought so, too."

He pulled at the knot and let the tie fall free to

the floor. "Do you think I should roll up my sleeves, or would that be too casual?"

He stretched to his full height.

Casual.

Nothing he ever did with Glory was casual. He'd always been good with people, especially women.

Glory Weston was definitely the exception to the rule. She was the most straightforward woman Ethan had ever known.

And yet with him, her yes was no, and her no, yes.

Which was why, he guessed, she'd called him up three days after she'd turned him down and told him she'd take him up on his offer.

He wouldn't look a gift horse in the mouth. Whether it was as a result of Ginger's prodding or a decision Glory had come to on her own, he was going to take advantage of the situation.

He'd promised to show her a good time, and with Meggie at his side, he most certainly would. He'd treat both his ladies like the princesses they were.

Of course, Glory, A-type personality that she was, would be mortified to discover he really didn't have any *precise* plans where the day was concerned.

She would want to plan every millisecond, know exactly where she was going, and when she would get there.

But he wasn't going to tell her of his plans, or lack thereof. He hadn't figured much past going to Puget Sound. What Glory needed was the fresh sting of saltwater, a dab of sunshine and a few flowers thrown in for effect.

He had a general plan. They'd catch an outgoing ferry to whatever island it was headed for, and let the rest of the day take care of itself.

It always did, in his experience.

The important thing was that, planned or unplanned, he'd be with Glory. He'd have the whole, complete, wonderful day with her all to himself. He hadn't looked forward to anything like this since he was a kid going to Disneyland. Come to think of it, Glory was even better.

He grinned at Meggie and swept her into his arms. "What do you think, kiddo? Your old man ready to get serious about a lady?"

"I can't believe you talked me into this," Glory complained, glaring at her sister's reflection in the vanity mirror. She winced as her sister pulled a section of her hair tight against her scalp.

"You're the one who decided to go out with Ethan, and you know it. I just had to nudge you a little to make the right decision."

"Do the words *invasion of privacy* mean anything to you?" she teased.

Ginger burst into melodious laughter, one of many traits Glory envied in her. "Oh, yeah, right. That's why you called me as soon as you got home that night. So you could protect your *privacy*."

"Point well taken."

Biting her lower lip, Ginger pulled up another strand of Glory's hair and then bent to survey her reflection in the mirror.

"Ouch! Watch it with the hair." Glory made a face at her sister's reflection. "If you pull any harder you're going to pull all my hair out."

"*You* were the one who wanted a French braid. If you'd gone wash-and-wear, you wouldn't be making weird faces at me."

"Ethan has seen me wash-and-wear. I wanted something a little different for this...um...outing."

"Date. It's called a *date*, Glory."

"This isn't a date." Glory shifted in her seat, afraid to give in to the moment, especially with her sister here.

Hope welled in her nonetheless. *Oh, heavenly*

Father, she prayed silently. *Do I really dare to hope Ethan might be the one?*

The one. The very thought took her breath away.

She did her best to hide the flush that rose to her cheeks, but with little expectation of success. Ginger noticed everything.

Everything.

"He asked you out in a supply closet, for pity's sake. Give it up, sis. I'm on to you."

Glory wanted to laugh. Ginger had continued their conversation without missing a beat, while she herself was having major personal revelations that felt like fireworks blasting.

Or maybe that was why Ginger chattered on, not that chattering was an extraordinary characteristic for Ginger.

Suddenly and spontaneously, Glory stood and turned, embracing her sister for all she was worth, and trying hard not to cry on her shoulder. She wouldn't want to ruin the great makeup job Ginger had done in her sudden rush of happiness.

She just wanted to share what she felt, but couldn't say it out loud.

She expected Ginger to pull away after a moment, but instead, she found herself in an embrace every bit as tight and fervent as her own. And to her very great surprise, the tears being shed were a surprisingly mute Ginger's.

Chapter Eight

"Honk!" The animated toddler flapped her arms and legs in excitement. "Honk, Papa Ethan. Honk!"

Ethan slipped Glory an amused glance and then smiled patronizingly at Meggie. His convertible was right in the middle of bumper-to-bumper traffic four cars across and at least ten deep.

"We have to wait for the boat, sweetie."

Meggie pointed at the dock. "Boat."

Clearly, she thought Papa Ethan was missing the obvious, and Ethan's smile widened as Glory chuckled under her breath.

"Blind, dumb or both?" he quipped.

"Ethan, that little girl obviously expects you to work miracles, as if you do it on a daily basis."

"Jesus is the only Miracle Worker, if my gray-haired Sunday school teacher has anything to say about it."

Glory nearly sat up straight in her seat. Ethan had said Jesus *is* the Miracle Worker.

Is. Maybe Ethan Wheeler's heart wasn't as hard as he thought.

She looked out over the broad dock and into Puget Sound. The sun was glimmering off the water in a way that made Glory's heart dance.

"When do we get in line for the boat?" she asked, adding quickly as an afterthought, "Not that I'm in a hurry or anything."

Ethan's gale of laughter was backed securely by the glow of amusement in his eyes. "We *are* in line."

Glory raised a brow.

"How so?" she asked, thinking the sailors on the dock might call them by rows of automobiles. Or maybe Ethan had a ticket.

She longed to get some fresh air while they were waiting to load. The convertible was nice, but kind of cramped to be sitting for so long. She wanted to experience nature, not man-made steel.

"Don't they have a waiting area outside? The weather is so lovely today. I hate to miss it."

Ethan chuckled again. "We'll be off in a moment.'' Suddenly he turned to her, his expression serious. ''Glory, how long have you lived in Seattle?''

''Three years. Why?''

''And how many times in those three years have you been to see the ocean?''

She'd been wondering at his line of thought, and suddenly it was clear. He was going to get on her case just like Ginger did.

She felt her heart, which had moments before been rejoicing in the day, fill with discouragement.

''Glory?'' He reached across the seat and softly brushed her hair away from her face.

''All right, already,'' she snapped, crossing her arms over her chest and desperately wishing she'd never agreed to come. ''I've never been to the ocean. Is that such a crime? I don't like seafood. I didn't see the point of going.''

She hated that she'd put in those last words. It sounded as if she were trying to justify herself, which she wasn't.

Not that it mattered. Ethan was otherwise engaged. He'd started the ignition and was slowly following the car in front of him down to the edge of the dock.

''The whole car goes onto the ferry?'' she

asked in astonishment, knowing she sounded a little like a kid with a new discovery.

The cars were going line by line into the bowels of the ship, which, she discovered, were more than large enough to handle them.

Which brought Glory to another discovery, this one not so fine. "Ethan, I'm claustrophobic."

He chuckled loudly. "We're in a convertible, remember?"

His hand still rested against her cheek, and he reached behind her, lightly tickling the back of her neck with his fingers. "Don't worry, gorgeous, we don't have to stay in the car."

"You'll never know how glad I am to hear you say that."

Impetuously, she reached back behind her and laid her hand over his, giving his fingers a light squeeze.

He, in turn, immediately pulled both their hands over her head and down between them on the car seat, where he gently laced their fingers.

Glory swept in a surprised breath, resisting the automatic urge to pull away.

It had been a long time since she'd held hands with a man. Her urge to pull away was fight or flight, she supposed. But she wondered if holding hands with Ethan meant the same thing that holding hands with a boy did when she was younger.

She certainly hoped so.

At Ethan's direction, the three of them exited his car and made their way up the stairs to the top of the ferry, where Ethan promised she could look out over the bow and breathe in the tangy salt air. After a tour of the boat and a snack, the three of them found a place to stand next to the railing.

Glory didn't think the ferry was moving very quickly, but nevertheless, the salt spray hit her face as she leaned out over the edge of the railing. She took a deep breath of the air and gasped in delight.

Ethan, bouncing Meggie on his arm to keep her occupied, watched Glory enjoy her first taste of the sea. He smiled, a smile that came from the very depths of his heart and soul.

What was it about Glory that made him want to wrestle the world into submission and hand it to her on a platter?

Glory whirled, her arms open as if for an embrace. Her green eyes were sparkling, her short, wispy red hair framing her head like a halo. "Oh, Ethan, it was just as you said it would be."

He chuckled. "I'm glad you like it. And remember, the day is only beginning!"

"Not to inflate your ego, hon," she said, winking at him in a way that made him want to do back flips, "but you must know you've created a fairy tale here. I can't wait to see what you've got planned next."

He cleared his throat. "Planned...yes, well...."

He was saved by the sound of horns bellowing that they would soon be approaching the dock.

"Belowdecks, me swabbies," he barked, tickling Meggie's tummy as she wiggled and giggled in his arms. "We're about to dock and deploy. Let the fairy tale commence."

By the time they'd reached Ethan's car, the troops were, in fact, disembarking for fairer shores. Ethan had been secretive and close-mouthed about what they'd be doing on the island, which he refused to tell her the name of, even.

He told her he wanted to keep a bit of mystery in the day, which only served to make Glory more curious, and to increase her anticipation. Which, she supposed, was the point.

The island was green, as was all of the Seattle area, but the little island gave her a sense of being all alone in the world. Well, almost all alone, and thank God for that. She wouldn't want to discount Ethan and Meggie for the world.

"My goodness," she commented as they moved away from where they'd parked.

It was one thing to hear Ethan say they could walk around the island without the use of a vehicle, but it was quite another thing to see it was so.

"That's all you're going to say?" Ethan quipped back. "My goodness?"

He shook his head and laughed. "Should I duck and run for cover?"

She punched him playfully on the arm, and he howled accordingly.

"Cut it out, silly. I was just thinking about how the seclusion of an island kind of gives you the feeling of being able to shirk off all your worries, all your stress, you know?"

He swung his arm around her shoulders so tight that he could bend his elbow, then pulled her forehead to his.

For a moment, he didn't speak, though his mouth made that cute little pucker that was half a smile and half an indication he was thinking of speaking.

"I'm glad," he murmured at last, and then the next instant he was rushing ahead of her, swinging Meggie around and calling for Glory to hurry up and follow him up a rather steep hill.

"Things to do, places to go, people to meet. Hurry up, and don't be late!"

She knew he was teasing her, but for some funny reason, his words made her feel better than she had in years.

Maybe ever.

To Ethan's very great surprise, the fact that he didn't have a plan didn't appear to bother Glory. A new, spontaneous woman was born as they walked, talked and laughed.

Or maybe her spontaneity wasn't new at all. Maybe she'd just suppressed it.

Now he was sounding like a psychiatrist or something. Next he'd be analyzing what she ate for breakfast.

But he was sorry to see the day end.

He leaned over the railing of the ferry and took a deep breath, enjoying the cool spray. Though the Seattle area in general stayed moderately comfortable year-round, the humidity still had him sweating, especially with all the walking they'd done.

Glory—and Meggie, in her own little way— wanted to see everything, walk every inch of the island, and most especially, to check out every little shop. Glory had swept Meggie away several times to inspect the toy aisles.

He, apparently, had been brought along to carry packages, he thought, unable to keep the grin from his face.

Women!

He moved to where Glory and Meggie were sharing a double-chocolate ice-cream cone. As he sat down beside Glory and dropped a casual arm around her, he wondered which of his sweet ladies was enjoying the treat more.

"So which part did you like best?"

He could feel the shuddering motion of Glory's shoulders as she chuckled softly. "If you're asking Meggie, I think she would have to say this yummy ice-cream cone."

He leaned close to her neck, inhaling the soft, floral scent that was Glory Weston.

"I was asking *you*," he whispered, able to feel his own breath off her skin. How close his lips were to the delicate skin beneath them. How sensitive each nerve felt as he considered the taste and feel of her skin beneath his lips.

With all his might, he pinched his lips together and pulled back, removing his arm from her and leaning hard on his elbows, clasping his hands in his lap.

Glory didn't move for a moment, then became intensely animated, bouncing Meggie on her knee and scrunching her face to look as if she were seriously contemplating his question about the day.

He knew, in fact, that she wasn't—at least, if their closeness affected her as much as it had affected him.

"I can't decide whether it was the kite flying or—" she paused to look contemplative "—the clam chowder. Yes, definitely the clam chowder."

Ethan barked out a laugh. "Yeah, Miss I-hate-fish-so-why-should-I-see-the-ocean Weston. Have you ever actually *had* fish before today?"

She shoved her chin in the air and looked offended. "Your father," she told the little girl on her lap, "is incorrigible. Completely incorrigible."

Ethan shook his head. "We've established that. And you're avoiding the issue."

Glory leaned in close, looking him right in the eye. He could smell her perfume again, and wondered why he'd never noticed or been affected by a woman's scent before, as he did Glory's.

"I *hate* fish. I have *tasted* fish, and I absolutely,

positively, beyond a shadow of a doubt *hate* fish.''

He grinned. ''Okay, then. It sounds as if maybe I've hit a soft spot with you?''

''I'm sorry, Ethan,'' she immediately apologized, looking genuinely contrite and pulling away from their duel of gazes.

''Hey, I was only kidding.''

She made a sound that was half a laugh and half a groan. ''I know you were.''

He could take offense to that comment, especially the way she said it, but he wouldn't. Not when there was something bothering Glory.

''I promise I won't take you to a seafood restaurant.''

Glory's gaze flashed back to Ethan. His statement could have been a joke, and probably was, however mistimed. But she didn't think so. For once, Ethan Wheeler was being completely serious.

Which left her to explain *her* outburst.

''People are allowed to dislike certain foods, but for some reason when I indicate my preferences, people always assume I've never tried fish. I guess maybe fish is one of those things like asparagus and broccoli that most kids hate, but eventually learn to like when they've grown up.''

"So what you're telling me is that you haven't grown up."

Laughter burst from her before she could stop it.

"Yeah, right. That's it." She shook her head. "I've been accused of a lot of things, but never not growing up."

When the boat horn suddenly sounded, she jumped and exclaimed in surprise.

"Time to go home," she said, wondering if she sounded as disappointed as she felt. It truly had been an exceptional day. One she'd treasure always.

Ethan swept Meggie to his shoulder, helped Glory to her feet, and laced his fingers with hers. "Don't worry, sweet Glory," he whispered for her ears only as he led them down the stairs to his car. "The fairy tale is just beginning."

She thought about his comment all the way back to the shelter, where she insisted he drop her off, knowing her sister would give her a ride home. She had a mile-high stack of paperwork to do and....

A fairy tale.

She smiled softly. Why did she suddenly believe dreams just might come true?

Ethan shut down his convertible before the shelter and insisted on walking her to the door.

"Will Meggie be okay by herself?"

"She'll be fine for a minute," Ethan said next to her ear. "I've rolled her window half down, and I'm not going very far."

He grinned widely as they stopped before the door. He reached for both her hands. "Thanks for worrying about Meggie. I'm glad you care."

"Of course, I care. She's such a sweet, wonderful little girl."

He stepped closer. "Is Meggie the only one you care for?"

Glory felt herself turning every shade of red, but he wouldn't let her turn away, pulling her closer, his eyes sparkling to match his ever present grin.

"Who else?" he whispered, leaning in close.

"Okay," she admitted in a squeak, trying to look anywhere but at Ethan's face. "You."

She leaned back against the door, realizing too late she couldn't move away. Then again, maybe subconsciously she didn't want to move away.

"Just a little bit?"

One arm snaked over her, creating a shady shelter—or a steel beam against her moving to the right. She voted for the latter when he leaned even closer.

"A...lot." She wasn't sure her voice was audible, for the raging sound of her blood in her ears.

"Well," he said, hovering just over her lips, "I happen to care about you...a lot...too."

Glory closed her eyes. This was the moment she'd been dreading, and much more the moment she'd been waiting for maybe for her whole life. She could feel his breath on her cheek, and stopped breathing herself.

"Open your eyes."

Her eyes snapped open. "What?"

He grinned. "I want you to see the man you're kissing."

"Oh." She didn't know what else to say. This time, when he leaned into her, she was ready. She even leaned forward, into the space his lips would soon occupy.

Their lips.

But just as his lips brushed hers and the world began to spin, the door behind them opened.

With his arms wrapped tightly around her, they fell into the front room of the shelter, Ethan carefully twisting them so that he'd take the brunt of the fall.

A dozen pairs of eyes were looking down on them. She would have shriveled in embarrassment, were it not that every gaze, even Ginger's, was deadly serious.

It was only a split second from spinning and falling that she caught the group's emotions.

She scrambled to her feet and whirled around to face her sister. "What? What happened? What's wrong? Ginger, tell me."

Ginger grimaced. "Glory, I hate to cut your day off short on account of us, but we have a...problem."

Chapter Nine

$\sim$

Ethan stood, brushed off his jeans, and put a firm, comforting arm around Glory before facing the crowd. "What's up?"

Lena stepped forward. Her eyes looked like a deer caught in headlights, but her expression was cool and determined. "Mark was here."

"What?" Glory jumped out of Ethan's arms. "What do you mean Mark was *here?* At the shelter?"

Ethan was out the door as fast as he'd fallen in, returning moments later with a sleeping Meggie tucked safely in his arms.

He kissed Meggie's forehead tenderly, then turned to the other women. "Tell me everything.

From the beginning. Every single detail that might be important later on.''

Ginger chuckled dryly. ''You sound like a cop.''

Glory lowered her gaze on Ginger, who shrugged. ''A good cop,'' she amended.

Ethan paced back and forth as he listened to the sisters tease each other, and attempted to think through the dilemma. ''A cop,'' he said softly, and then louder, ''Hey, that's not a bad idea. Did someone call the police?''

''They won't do anything,'' Glory stated.

He wondered how she could be so sure of herself when she didn't know all the facts, but he didn't voice the question aloud. She'd already taken charge of the situation, and she was really very good at it.

He couldn't help but admire her strength and calm, and how her attitude radiated among the group of obviously shaken, if not terrified, women.

''Exactly,'' said a young blond woman toting a baby on her hip. ''There's a restraining order on Mark, so they could technically come and haul him off if he was making a scene here, but Mark's too smart for that.''

''What happened?'' Ethan asked again. He was surprised when it was Lena who answered.

''Mark played the oldest trick in the book. I mean, it's been on television a million times. He came dressed as a computer specialist. Said he was here to fix one of our computers.'' She shivered.

Ethan felt like shivering, too. ''How'd he know about the computers?''

''It's hard to say,'' Glory answered. ''He's obviously keeping a pretty close watch on us, but we don't know how he does it.''

''Did you let him in?''

Ginger snorted. ''I may be blond, but I'm not stupid. I sent him packing in a second.''

''Didn't that make him angry?''

''He's always angry.'' Lena made a choking sound. ''He's also smooth as butter. Good-looking, mild-mannered. The kind of guy you'd let in the front door if you didn't know better.''

Ethan opened his arms to Lena. He wasn't sure she'd be wanting any contact with a man so soon after this incident, but she also looked frazzled and alone.

To his surprise, though, she accepted his proffered hug, and he offered her what comfort he could.

He wanted to do so much for her—for all the women here at Angel's Wings. And right now, he wanted to knock Mark's lights out.

These women were all putting on a brave face, but a casual observer could tell they were scared to death. And rightly so, Ethan thought, clenching his fist despite his best efforts to the contrary.

These were *his* women.

Glory was writing frantically on a clipboard, and Ginger was dancing distractedly from foot to foot.

"I'm really sorry, sis," she said quietly, for Glory's ears only. Ethan looked away, not letting on that he'd heard.

Glory shook her head and frowned. "It's not your fault. Mark made the advance, not you. You couldn't have known."

She hugged her sister tight. "I shouldn't have left the shelter. I knew better. It was my mistake."

Ethan felt his heart drop like lead into his stomach. They'd encountered a very serious situation, and he'd do everything within his power to make sure it didn't happen again.

But he hurt like he'd never hurt before when Glory had so quickly brushed off their day together. A stabbing pain emanated from his chest, in the general vicinity of his heart.

She'd called it a mistake.

Their fairy-tale day. A mistake.

But there was no doubt Glory meant what she said. She quickly hustled the shelter women away, getting them busy at this task or that, or simply and quietly suggesting they return to their rooms.

When only he, Glory and Ginger remained, Glory ushered them into the office, where she did most of her paperwork. Sitting behind her desk, she steepled her fingers and shifted her gaze from Ethan to Ginger and back.

Ethan smiled, but Glory's expression was cold and unreadable.

He swallowed hard. She looked at him— through him—as if he were simply an employee, a casual acquaintance.

Or maybe a complete stranger.

The woman he saw staring back at him didn't believe in fairy tales.

His throat pinched tighter.

"Well?" Ginger finally asked, after a prolonged silence. "I'm assuming we're supposed to be coming up with solutions to our current crisis."

Ethan silently thanked Ginger for taking the initiative.

Glory laid her hands flat on the table and leaned forward. "Do you have any solutions?"

The room faded into uncomfortable silence. They all looked at one another, but no words were said.

After an extended moment, Ethan cleared his throat. "I, um...do."

Both women stared at him in surprise.

"Why are you surprised? You think I don't know anything about what's happening?"

Glory lifted one eyebrow.

"Okay, well, maybe not. But I have a question, at least."

"Shoot," said both sisters simultaneously, a sisterly inclination which made him want to smile deep down.

"Couldn't we beef up the level of security around here?"

Before they could answer, he continued. "Actually, my question is really, what *is* the current level of security around here? I haven't seen any. Security, that is."

He felt as if Glory were glaring at him, although, considering the turn of events, he might be wrong. Still....

"I'm not criticizing what you've done here,

Glory. I'm just trying to figure out how to fix the current problem."

Ginger barked a laugh, breaking into the tension in the room. "Isn't that just like a man? Everything that's been going on around him, and he wants to *fix the problem.*"

Ethan raised both eyebrows and set his arms akimbo. "You want to talk about our feelings?"

Even Glory laughed at that one, but only for a moment.

"Sit down, Ethan," she said, sweeping an encouraging hand at a folded chair leaning against the wall. "You, too, sis. We may be here awhile."

Obligingly, Ethan unfolded a chair for Ginger, then took one for himself and turned it backward before sitting down, so he could lean his arms against the chair back.

"Our security," Glory began, "must, by necessity, remain loose."

"I don't understand," he said softly.

Glory smiled, almost indulgently. "If we put up tall fences and barbed wire around the place, it'd be a dead giveaway that this isn't just any normal, if somewhat wealthy, home set apart from the bustle of the city. Bells and whistles."

"Yeah," agreed Ginger. "Besides, barbed wire

or some such might make the ladies feel like they were in prison, you know?''

Ethan chuckled, though he didn't really feel the mirth. "You ladies are making fun of me."

"Of course," said Ginger.

"Not really, Ethan," said Glory at the same time.

He shrugged. "Which is it?"

"I was exaggerating with the barbed wire, but I had a point."

"Machine guns aside, couldn't you at least hire security guards to patrol the surrounding area? Even unarmed guards would help, I think, though I'd recommend the armed variety."

"Perhaps," Glory agreed with a nod. "But then again, those same guards, who'd no doubt make some women feel safe, would also remind others just how much they've fallen from a normal, sane lifestyle."

"Yes, but they're hiding from potentially violent husbands," he contended, gripping the chair back with his fists.

"Most of these guys won't ever *actually* pursue their wives or girlfriends to a shelter," Ginger explained quietly. "After the initial, critical few days, most guys give up and go on to seek greener pastures.

"But the women here have to go on, and hopefully not into another abusive relationship. That's where Angel's Wings can really help. Especially thanks to your new computers."

"They're your computers," he answered automatically. "So most guys give up, but there are a few Marks out there who can't give it up."

"Unfortunately, he's not the first man to make an issue out of his wife and children being here. There are shelters more conducive to those who know they're being pursued."

She shook her head sadly. "It looks like we may have to move Lena and Stephen and Mary to another shelter."

Ethan nodded. "I'll help. But I don't understand why they weren't moved before. Everyone seemed to know who Mark was, and to look out for him, which means this wasn't the first assault, was it?"

Glory sighed. Ethan was so zealous and fervent about every little thing. And she was tired. Very, very tired.

"I've been trying to get them to move, ever since he started sending letters and threatening notes to the shelter address.

"Unfortunately, Lena's a stubborn woman, and she doesn't want to leave. She says she's tired of feeling like a fox on the hunt, running from borough to borough every time she hears the bay of the hunter's dogs, and the bugle of the hunter's horn.''

"I can see her point."

He would see her point, of course. She glanced tiredly at her sister, and then back to Ethan. ''Hopefully, she'll change her mind now that he's actually come to the shelter.''

"More people than just Lena could get hurt in all this,'' Ginger pointed out grimly, before kissing Glory on the cheek and saying her goodbyes to both of them, having a prior engagement to teach at a university. "You know I'm talking truth here, Glory.

"You've got to do something. But I'll leave you two to figure it out. I have the highest confidence in you both.'' She chuckled tiredly, then was gone.

Glory leaned back in her chair. Even the familiar nip and squeak of the springs didn't comfort her. Not the familiar smell of fresh-cut flowers. Not even the smooth, slick feel of her old desk under her palms.

The weight of responsibility shifted heavily on her shoulders, and she called out silently to God.

How could she possibly protect all these women? How could one woman....

Ethan leaned over her desk and picked up her creased, brown leather Bible. He ran a hand across the cover, then rifled through the pages.

"You can't protect them all, Glory," he said so softly she wondered for a moment if she'd heard him right.

The next instant she wondered, mortified, if she'd spoken her private prayer aloud.

Had Ethan heard her?

Wanting to avoid his gaze, she looked up and met his kind blue eyes instead. The usual bright amusement was missing, but in its place was a deep, burning intensity that both alarmed her and reassured her, a true paradox indeed.

"I can tell what you're thinking," he explained, and relief that she hadn't spoken her prayer aloud burst out of her lungs in a rush of air.

"I have to try," was her only response. So few words, yet the very core and soul of her being met behind them. This was what she was here for, her reason for living.

"*We* have to try," he corrected gently. "And that's not what I meant. I'll be walking beside you every step of the way with this Mark guy. You won't ever be alone.

"But I think...I think the battle is greater than just Mark, or Pete or any other jerk who batters his wife."

She waited wordlessly for him to continue, guessing—no, *hoping*—to hear the words of comfort she so needed right now.

"God is on your side, Glory."

He placed the Bible gently on the table and once again ran his hand across the cover, brushing his fingers over the gold inscription.

"*Holy Bible.* I wish I remembered the verses I learned as a child."

He closed his eyes and bowed his head. "I *know* God wants to protect us. And Lena. I just don't know where to find the verses that say so."

Glory stood and crossed around the table so she could put her arm around Ethan. She brushed her fingers through his soft, fine blond hair, taking comfort in his presence and his words.

"Do you remember the story of the Good Shepherd, Ethan?" she asked softly.

He nodded, and the smile that lit her day returned to his face.

"The Bible talks a lot about Jesus being our

Shepherd. My favorite verse is from the prophet
Isaiah:

> He shall lead His flock like a Shepherd,
> He shall gather the lambs in His arms,
> And carry them in His bosom,
> And gently lead those who are with young.

When I'm afraid or overwhelmed, I simply picture the sweet women and children in Angel's
Wings as the lambs in His arms, the little ones
tucked right on up next to His heart.''

"What about you?" Ethan whispered, reaching
for her hand. "Do you see yourself as a lamb in
the Master's arms?"

The question nearly knocked Glory off her feet,
and blew the air right out of her lungs.

She was a Christian, of course. But there were
so many souls so much needier than her own, that
she rarely considered herself in the equation.

"You are, you know," Ethan said, standing.
He placed a soft kiss on her forehead, then
wrapped his arms tight around her as if he would
never let go. "My sweet Glory. Jesus's little
lamb."

Chapter Ten

Glory had just curled up on her blue gingham sofa with a cup of hot cinnamon tea. She was glad to be home. It had been a long day, and for once, she was seeking refuge in a place away from the shelter.

She hadn't turned on the television, though the radio was playing soft Celtic hymns in the background.

She was too busy thinking about the past week at the shelter to truly relax. This day alone had been one of the roughest she'd had in her time as the shelter's director.

Of course she'd had to deal with overbearing, angry husbands a few times in the past few years, but she had never felt the sense of imminent danger to the shelter and its occupants the way she did now.

Lena sure wasn't making it easy for her.

She'd thought Mark showing up would have her begging to be transferred to another shelter; if not for herself, for her son Stephen and little daughter Mary.

But Lena was more adamant than ever. She'd put her back up and wouldn't budge an inch.

She wasn't going to leave. She was finished running scared.

While Glory admired her strength and spirit in the face of adversity, she wondered if Lena had thought her decision completely through. Did she understand that she and her children weren't the only ones at risk if Mark became enraged?

She should have pointed it out to Lena. And she would have, but she didn't want to play on the woman's fear. Though Lena would never openly admit it, she really *was* afraid.

And with good reason, Glory thought with a shudder.

Oh, to be as strong, both in spirit and in faith, as Lena daily demonstrated. Glory's own faithfulness and commitment paled before hers. She'd never experienced anything remotely as terrifying as what Lena had gone through with Mark.

In the end, she'd knelt with Lena in prayer for rest, peace and safety for her and her children, and prayed that Mark would give up his quest to seek vengeance on Lena and leave her alone.

The thought of Mark returning left Glory thoroughly chilled. She brought her still-steaming mug of tea to her lips and took a tentative sip.

Just then, someone knocked loudly on her door. Glory nearly jumped out of her skin. Tea splashed onto her lap, and she yelped in pain. Sweatpants did precious little to shield her skin from the scalding liquid, she thought, as she quickly wiped the drops away with her fingers.

Placing her mug on a coaster on her oak end table, she put her palm to her chest to still her erratically racing heart. Then she shook her head and laughed quietly at her quaky nerves.

It wasn't too smart, thinking about danger, her own vulnerability, and the present menace of Lena's husband this late at night and while she was alone, even if she was far from the shelter.

Still, the knock surprised Glory. She hadn't ordered food delivered, and relatively few people knew where she lived, leastwise many acquaintances in the Kirkland area, the location of her personal town house, which she used primarily on weekends and when she'd spent the whole day at the corporate office in Seattle.

Generally, she preferred to sleep at the shelter, so she could work as late as she wanted without having to worry about driving anywhere. The paperwork involved in running a shelter was phenomenal, and she never really felt caught up.

Maybe it was Ginger, though she rarely visited without calling first. Besides, unlike Glory, Ginger had an active nightlife, and it *was* Friday night. Her sister would be out on a date.

She cautiously opened the door partway without releasing the chain lock. "Hello?"

"Surprise!" Ethan stuck his nose in the gap, and Glory jumped back, laughing.

"Ethan. What are you doing here?"

After she'd spoken, she realized how rude she sounded, and because she hadn't meant it that way, she immediately and falteringly amended her statement. "I'm really glad to see you. It's just that you're an unexpected surprise. A nice, unexpected surprise."

Ethan chuckled and flashed her a toothy grin. "I'm glad to hear you say so. I like giving you surprises, but I like being one even more."

He was relieved she wasn't angry. He hadn't

known if she'd want to see him, especially since his visit was completely unannounced and it was fairly late.

He was severely breaching the embodiment of his childhood country manners to make a house call after nine o'clock in the evening. His older brother Erik, who'd raised him, would be ashamed of his rude conduct.

But Ethan was bouncing with enthusiasm, and he just couldn't wait until tomorrow.

"Are you going to let me in? I come bearing gifts. Well, I have one gift, anyway."

Glory slammed the door—almost what he would consider in his face, he noted, but she hastily removed the chain lock, so he forgave her.

"Ethan, you don't have to bring a gift every time you see me."

"Don't worry, gorgeous, the gift is for the shelter." He stepped into the door, a pajama-clad, sleeping Meggie in his arms.

"Is it chocolate?"

He grinned and shook his head. "Not this time. Do you have a blanket or something I could lay on the floor for Meggie?"

"The *floor?*"

Glory sounded absolutely appalled, and Ethan cringed, wondering what he'd said wrong now.

"Ethan Wheeler, I'm not going to put that precious child on the *floor*."

He shrugged uncomfortably. He put Meggie on the floor all the time, with blankets underneath her, of course. And he always snuggled her up tight.

But he sure didn't want to admit to it, in case it really was the wrong thing to do. He didn't exactly have a handbook for parenting toddlers. How was he supposed to know what to do?

He'd thought he was doing all right, but....

"Will she fall off my bed, do you think?" Glory asked, pacing from one end of the room to the other, worrying her bottom lip with her teeth as she walked. "I don't have a crib, and I don't know anyone I can borrow one from. But I don't know if she'll be safe on my bed or not."

Ethan pursed his lips, then grinned widely. "That's why I put her on the floor."

To his surprise, Glory laughed. "Okay. I'll get some blankets."

In moments, they had Meggie comfortably ensconced on the floor by the sofa. Ethan gently placed Meggie's blankie over her small body and brushed her hair back from her face.

"My bright little starburst," he said softly.

No matter how much time he spent with Meggie, his heart still welled whenever he watched her peacefully sleeping. What a blessing he'd been given.

Glory rubbed a hand across his back. He looked up, smiling, to see her looking at Meggie with much the same expression as he imagined he had, only he thought it looked much better on the beautiful redhead with sparkling green eyes and a heart-soaring smile.

That is, when he could get her to smile, which wasn't often enough for his liking. Not *nearly* often enough.

She was smiling now. "Do you want to tell me about her?" she whispered, her voice soft and silky smooth.

Suddenly he very much wanted to tell her.

"How did you know there was a story?"

"A single man raising a baby girl not his own? There's a story." She smiled tenderly. "Is she your niece?"

Ethan laughed, and realized how bitter it sounded. "No. Nothing as simple as that, though we're related by blood."

Glory only leaned back onto the couch in answer, tucking her legs beneath her.

"My cousin Sabrina and I met quite by accident in law school. My immediate family is just me and my two brothers. I didn't know we even had cousins. And then Sabrina and I met, and became good friends.''

He wasn't sure he'd be able to get through this, but he gritted his teeth and continued. ''She was married to a batterer. She kept hoping Jason would change, but then she had Meggie, and the stakes changed.''

Glory reached out and laced her fingers through his, giving his hand a light squeeze of comfort.

''I tried to get her away. I swear I did. But on the night we'd chosen to sneak her away, Jason discovered and—'' he pounded his free fist into her couch ''—killed Sabrina.''

''And you got Meggie?''

''Jason went to jail, and I appealed to the courts to be the next logical choice of kin. Though I was ready to fight tooth and nail to get Meggie. Sometimes I think she's my reason for living.''

''And the reason I was so graciously visited by you regarding a donation,'' Glory said, putting the pieces together.

''That's right.''

''I know you aren't going to listen to me, but I'm going to say it anyway. It's not your fault, Ethan. There was nothing you could do to change the events as they happened.

"You are, in fact, quite amazing. Not many men would take on a toddler. And there's not a person alive who could fault you for your job parenting Meggie."

Ethan winced, knowing there were probably many ways he failed in parenting that he didn't even know about.

"Moving back to happier subjects," she said with a silky laugh, "Where's my surprise?"

"I'll go get him," Ethan answered promptly, trying to swallow around the catch in his throat.

"Him?"

He cringed at the slip of his tongue, and to Glory's could-be negative reaction to it.

"Uh...I don't think I want to try to explain him to you. Just stay put and I'll be right back. No preconceived notions, okay?"

He walked back outside and pulled in a deep, fortifying breath of air. The night was cool, but he'd broken into a sweat, which he carefully wiped off with his handkerchief.

"Oh, this wasn't a good idea, Wheeler," he said aloud in a rush of breath. "In fact, I think this is the worst idea you've ever had."

And that was really saying something.

He stopped before the shiny new silver minivan

he'd purchased earlier that day and grimaced, both at his predicament and the minivan itself.

What had possessed him to buy the quintessential family car? And the crazy thing was his answer—it was Glory every bit as much as it was Meggie.

Propping his elbow on the rooftop, he leaned his head against his hand and groaned.

What was he doing lately? And why? He'd never been more confused in his life.

Two months ago he was a tightly wired corporate executive putting all his time and energy into his law firm, with his only real touch to humanity being his sweet Meggie.

He'd known where he was supposed to go, what he was supposed to do, and how he was supposed to act.

Now, more often than not, his legal assistants pulled most of the weight in the firm, while he was off chasing his dreams.

And for all that, he'd moved into a state of chaos beyond imagining. He didn't know anything anymore, and it just kept getting worse.

He was leaning against a minivan, for crying out loud. It was laughable. Except that he didn't feel like laughing at all.

He'd seen the greatest happiness of his life

since the day he'd walked into the corporate office of Angel's Wings and proposed his wacky ideas for contributing computers. That one move had ended in his contributing nothing less than the total package—Ethan Wheeler, heart and soul.

He'd not thought to find happiness, not since the death of his cousin shattered all his illusions about finding happiness in marriage.

Then Glory entered his life and changed everything. Glory. And the shelter. The ladies and children there he was learning to love and who had given him a true sense of purpose and meaning he'd been direly lacking as they freely gave their own gift of love.

Battered. Wounded. But not broken.

And yet....

There was still something missing.

Not *missing,* exactly, merely hovering just out of his reach. He knew what it was. Or more precisely, *who* it was.

The workers at the shelter talked about Jesus Christ as if He were a friend, someone with whom they had a very personal relationship—a daily, constant experience, in stark contrast to his own infrequent, clumsy prayers to the Father.

Father, Son and Holy Spirit. He knew God. He

believed Jesus died for his sins. But the daily walk thing was a new concept.

He closed his eyes, but didn't pray, at least not with words.

Making a sound that was halfway between a sigh and a groan, he pushed himself off the van and opened the back hatch. "Hey, Bruno, how are you doing, boy?"

The pitch-black German shepherd inside the metal cage scratched eagerly at his confines and whined a happy hello.

"Yeah, I'll bet you'd like me to get you out of there."

He released the dog from his cage, slammed the hatch shut, and headed for the door, feeling as if he were walking the last dance before an execution.

Yet another harebrained scheme for Ethan Wheeler. And the crowd goes wild.

Glory opened the door when he knocked, and immediately exclaimed her surprise.

"A dog?" She took a shaky step backward, and Ethan moved forward to catch her elbow.

"I'm sorry," he apologized, his heart stricken. Why was he so impulsive? Just once, it would be nice if he thought things all the way through before he embarked onto one of his novelties.

"I didn't consider the possibility that you'd be afraid of dogs."

"Oh, I'm not," she said, crouching to the dog's level and allowing him to sniff her closely fisted hand before petting him. "I love dogs. You just surprised me."

Ethan pursed his lips and grinned crookedly. "That seems to be happening a lot lately."

"What's his name?"

"Bruno."

"Bruno? That sounds like a bulldog or a mastiff or something, not a German shepherd."

He winced. "I guess you're right. It is an odd name. But I'm not responsible. The name came with the dog."

"You got him from the pound?"

"Oh, no." Ethan shook his head. "I got him at—" he took a deep breath and pressed on "—at a professional dog-training center."

When she didn't scream in protest, he continued cautiously.

"You know, where they train police K-9 units and such."

That pulled a response from her. Her eyebrows hit her hairline, and then she frowned, her dark eyebrows scrunched endearingly together over her small, straight nose.

"What does that mean? That he is trained to be a fighting dog?"

"In a sense. He's been through several levels of training. He can track, run agility paths, sniff out drugs or people, and bring down a criminal, among other things."

Glory pinched her lips and looked away, but Ethan caught her expression before she did—like she wanted to cry. It ate him up inside.

Glory wasn't the crying type.

She cleared her throat and squared her shoulders. "I think I know where you're going with this. I'm sorry, Ethan, but I'm afraid I'm going to have to nix this particular idea right here and right now, before it gets out of control.

"I hope you understand, and that there will be no problem giving him back to his training center and getting a refund."

Ethan frowned, feeling as if he'd been punched in the gut. She was being totally unfair! And without even hearing the facts!

He'd expected resistance, but not an out-and-out refusal to even consider the matter. That was hardly reasonable.

Fortunately for him, he was a lawyer, and Bruno *was* a good idea. Glory just didn't know it yet.

But she would.

"Madame Director," he said in his best closing argument voice, "you have yet to examine the facts in this case. I'm sure if you'll consider the matter you'll see—"

"I won't see your point of view," she snapped, cutting him off.

"That wasn't what I was going to say," Ethan replied, confounded.

"No?"

"No. I was *going* to say that you haven't yet heard, much less examined, the facts in this case."

Glory blanched, then nodded apologetically. He was quite right. She hadn't let him say a word, much less explain why Bruno was here.

She owed him that, at least. He was a good friend, and she knew he had the best interests of the shelter in mind, however misguided his hare-brained scheme.

"You've tried and found me guilty, sir."

A moment ago he'd looked hurt and angry, but in a wink, or maybe that was *with* a wink, his expression returned to the old, cheerful Ethan she knew and loved, accompanied by that sweet little pucker that suggested a smile.

"Does that make me the judge? 'Cause if I get to deal out the punishment..."

His eyes were shining, and there was no mistaking his meaning.

A blush rose up her neck and into her face. It was an unfortunate aspect of being a redhead; the light, smooth skin that beamed like Rudolph's nose whenever she was embarrassed.

Part of her wanted to run and hide at his implications. How could he tease her this way?

Then again, running straight into his arms wasn't such a bad idea, either, as ideas went. She fought to suppress a grin.

"Would you like a cup of tea?" she offered, resisting the impulse to flee, or something worse and infinitely more problematic. "I have several herbal blends to choose from."

Ethan shook his head. "I'm a coffee man, myself. Tea isn't my cup. Not manly enough for my tastes, you know."

He grinned. "But don't feel obligated to make coffee on my account. I'll do just fine with a glass of water."

"I would feel blessed to make you coffee," she said, then colored at the awkward language she'd learned from her mother.

His smile made it all worthwhile, as he sauntered out of the kitchen, looking as if he had the world in his pocket.

Glad for something to keep her occupied for a moment, Glory set about to make a pot of coffee for Ethan while he wrestled quietly with Bruno on the rug.

It struck her that there was something oddly domestic about the situation—a man, a woman, a baby and a dog, all happily, contentedly together on a Friday night.

She shook her head. Her woolgathering was going to get her into trouble one of these days. She definitely ought to be thinking more about the big black dog, and less about the big, irrepressible man.

What in the world was she going to do with a German shepherd?

Because she was relatively certain Ethan was going to talk her into whatever outrageous scheme he had concocted. To her increasing chagrin, she found she couldn't say no to the man.

Who could resist him when he pursed his lips and cracked that crooked smile that made the sun shine?

And the dog was pretty charming, too.

Bringing a large mug of coffee to Ethan, she settled onto the sofa. Bruno immediately moved in her direction, placing his chin on her knee and looking up at her, pleading for attention with his big, black eyes.

"Oh, you men are all alike," she said, scratching the dog behind his ears.

"We all want attention?" Ethan asked, still crouching on the floor.

"No, I was thinking more about the puppy-dog look that helps you get your way."

Ethan sat down beside her on the sofa, his arm resting lightly over her shoulders. With his hand on her cheek, he gently turned her head until their gazes locked. His eyes were full of compassion and something else she didn't dare hope to recognize.

"I'm not trying to get my own way here," he said softly. "It's completely your decision, Glory, and I'll respect whatever you decide."

She sighed softly. "Remember, Ethan, whatever *I* think about Bruno, he has to be approved by the board of directors."

"How could I forget?" He grinned, his eyes sparkling. "I brought him here tonight because I wanted you to become acquainted with Bruno first. *Before* I made a formal proposal to the board."

Glory was ashamed of the way she had acted

earlier, jumping to conclusions before Ethan had a chance to say a word. She prayed for forgiveness. She had an exceptionally hard heart. God sometimes had to take a jackhammer to it.

"Ethan, I am *so* sorry. I acted like a complete dumbbell earlier. Will you forgive me?"

He looked surprised.

"I know what you're thinking. Glory Weston, the world's number one Frost Queen, coming down from her icy throne to apologize."

"Glory, I wasn't thinking anything of the sort," he protested rather loudly.

She shook her head. "I saw your face. I'm not blaming you. It's true."

"Glory." He took her by the shoulders and turned her to face him. "Be quiet for a minute."

She laughed, struggling *not* to struggle in his arms. He was holding her gently, but her flight instinct had kicked in nonetheless.

"I admit I was surprised, but not by your apology. I've never met a woman with more honor, dignity, strength, character and love as you have, or a woman that I've admired more.

"I was surprised because I've never had anyone ask me for forgiveness before. I—it—"

With a huff of breath, he cut off whatever it was he was going to say.

His blue eyes were blazing, sparkling stars. The myriad emotions in his gaze were beyond reading.

Glory struggled for something to say, but Ethan cut her off with a look.

She found herself leaning into his hand, which had slid up her shoulder to cup her jaw. His other hand slid around her back, pulling her closer.

"Glory, I—" he said, his voice raw and husky.

This time it was she who cut Ethan off. The cool, brisk scent of his aftershave, the sweet smell of his warm breath, and the burning look in his eyes all melted together to send her head spinning.

His lips were mere inches from hers. She closed the gap in an instant, freezing just as their lips met.

What was she doing?

Passing the point of no return.

Kissing the man she loved.

Chapter Eleven

~e~

It was as easy as that, and every bit much as difficult.

As Ethan deepened the kiss, murmuring sweet nothings under his breath, he knew he'd passed the point of no return. Glory might not know it, but his lips were sealing his intent. His commitment.

His love?

It was worth exploring, he thought, grinning over her lips.

"What's so funny?" she murmured, cuddling into his chest.

"Funny?"

"You were smiling."

"Of course I was smiling. I just kissed a beautiful woman."

"Thank you." He barely heard the words, muffled as they were by his T-shirt.

"Heh, heh," he said, trying to sound like the bad guy. "Anytime, gorgeous. Anytime."

She swatted him with her hand, and their camaraderie was instantly restored. Ethan was glad. As much as he wanted to keep kissing and snuggling all evening, they still had to deal with the subject of a very active, pacing Bruno.

"We have to talk about the dog," he reminded her regretfully.

"Okay," she said softly. "Talk away."

She yawned, then gestured her apology with her hand. "I'm listening."

"Don't let me keep you awake," he teased, chuckling loudly.

She covered her mouth over another yawn. "Don't worry. I won't crash on you. I'm just so...*comfortable* at the moment."

He hoped so, as she hadn't moved out of his embrace. He had her right where he wanted her, in the best sense of the words.

"I bought Bruno for the shelter."

He could feel her chuckle into his shirt. "I suspected as much."

"Then why did you say it wasn't a good idea?" In for a penny...

"Um, can I *not* answer on the grounds that it may incriminate me?"

"Not in this court."

She stretched, reminding Ethan of a cat, then wrapped her arms lazily around his neck, kissed his cheek, and snuggled into his side.

"Ethan, you're a wonderful, kind, caring man. But you do—occasionally—have the tendency to run off half-cocked in your enthusiasm to help out."

"I can see how someone might *possibly* think that about me." He tried to sound wounded, but didn't think he succeeded very well.

He wasn't going to admit to anything if he could avoid it. He pursed his lips in an attempt to keep from smiling.

"But what does that have to do with you and me?"

"You, me and Bruno here," she reminded him in a wry tone. "The fact of the matter is, we can't have a dog at the shelter, Ethan, no matter how much I'd like to accommodate you."

Why did he get the feeling she wasn't going to listen to his proposal? Her ears were closed.

He squeezed a tight fist in his frustration with

Glory. The woman swung as widely as a pendulum in her emotions and actions.

"Why not?" he asked, after an extended silence.

He wasn't usually silent, especially when he felt as strongly about an issue as he did about Bruno. But he didn't know what to say, didn't know how to convince her to at least give it a try.

Maybe it was having to approach the board of directors that was holding her back. But then again, she knew there was very little Ethan Wheeler couldn't get around if he put his mind to it.

If he could win Glory to his side....

"Why not?" she echoed his question, sounding as if he'd spoken the question in a foreign language.

"Why not? Well, for starters, a dog would be unsanitary. I can't have a big, slobbery dog wandering around the shelter. I have hygiene issues to think about.

"Another issue is, of course, safety. We have a number of children at the shelter, as you well know. Many of them are too little to be around such a big dog. What if he bit someone? Can you picture some of these problems here?"

Ethan shrugged, but she didn't let him talk.

"If I brought Bruno in, I'm sure it would cause a huge ruckus among the women living at Angel's Wings."

He sighed. "Are you finished yet?"

She clamped her mouth shut, her eyes wide, then nodded her answer to his question.

"Okay, then. Let's take these concerns of yours one by one."

He ticked them off on his fingers.

"First, hygiene. Bruno is a dog, not a walking, barking germ carrier. He's no more dangerous than you or me. If there's a kid with allergies or something, we could make allowances accordingly. He'd only be allowed in some of the public rooms, and would mostly remain outside doing his duty."

"Hmm," she said, absently stroking his jaw with her fingers, making it awfully hard to think about the matter at hand.

"Second," he continued, trying to ignore the feelings she stirred in him with every caress, "we don't necessarily have to have an inside dog at all, if that becomes a monumental problem."

"I don't understand."

Ethan blew out a breath. Why hadn't he started with the rationale behind getting Bruno in the first place? Or had he tried?

He grinned. It was time to start out with another round.

"I've been going over and over the problem of security at Angel's Wings, and until Bruno, I hadn't been able to come up with a solution."

"Security," she said, sounding surprised.

Ethan cocked his head at her and raised his eyebrows. "Of course. It's the perfect solution, even if I do say so myself. What, you thought I bought you a full-grown dog without asking you about it first? He's on loan, you know."

She pinched her lips wryly, as if holding back a smile. "Explain, you big lug."

She pushed away from him and pulled her legs up on the sofa, wrapping her arms around them. She looked adorably mussed as she pushed her hair back over her head and wiggled her bare feet.

His heart swelled in his chest.

Her expression, however, was suddenly all interest, and all business. Too bad!

"The training center allowed me to interact with several dogs, and there were more that I saw and didn't mingle with.

"I picked Bruno because the two of us hit it off right away. He's a tough old fellow, but he's got such a kindness in his eyes."

He stopped talking, and then added as an afterthought, "But there are other dogs."

"You said that."

"What I mean is, Bruno is an inside-outside dog. He's been especially socialized to small children, though all the dogs are well socialized to people of all ages.

"Bruno's supposed to go to a family, or to the police, since police dogs usually go home with the K-9 officer at night. You know, the kind of dog a criminal wouldn't know was specially trained until it was already too late."

He chuckled, and it bothered him that she didn't join him. He cleared his throat and continued.

"The dogs trained to be more suited to guarding large businesses, the outside dogs, are usually sold as a group, so they have regular canine interaction, if not human interaction. Those are the ones you see on television action movies—the ones patrolling the grounds with a bite worse than their barks.

"Either way, they have training classes for you to learn how guard dogs work, and how to work with them. If you decide in favor of Bruno, I'll sign you and the rest of your immediate staff up for lessons. We'll want to be careful how many people we have working specifically with Bruno, for security reasons.''

He stopped talking.

He didn't have anything else to say. His last sentence had been worded half as a joke, but Glory hadn't laughed. And it was terribly awkward to sit and watch Glory and not speak.

He rubbed his palms flat against the denim of his jeans and waited.

Her lips were tightly pinched and her brow low. She looked much like a young girl concentrating on drawing a picture.

Only there was no picture. Just his knee, if he interpreted the direction of her gaze correctly.

''Glory?''

She looked up slowly, her lips still pinched. But her green eyes were wide and clear. ''Well, I guess the best way to figure this all out is to have Bruno visit the shelter. The sooner the better. Tomorrow morning, I think. First thing. Is it a date?''

Ethan grinned so wide he thought his cheeks might burst. She was giving his idea a shot, probably against her better judgment.

In answer to her question, he stood and pulled her up into his hug.

''Thank you,'' he whispered into her neck, enjoying the feel of brushing his lips against her soft, fragrant skin. "You won't regret it."

Glory laughed and hugged him back. "I already do, you crazy, adorable man. I already do."

Chapter Twelve

"Cool. A dog," Ginger said as she met Ethan and Glory at the door. "What a great idea!"

Glory wasn't at all sure it was a great idea; in fact, she was inclined to think it was a pretty poor one, not to reflect badly on Ethan in any way.

It was simply a matter of bad judgment.

That, and the fact that she couldn't seem to say no to Ethan when she was face-to-face with him. He'd already pushed the envelope about as far as she would—or could—allow it to stretch.

She felt tired. She couldn't keep up with him.

Maybe that was the problem. How could she continue to focus on the day-to-day work and the worries of running the shelter if she was going to be continually distracted by Ethan's latest notions?

And Ethan himself, she admitted reluctantly. She grew weary just thinking about the innumerable possibilities.

"Yes, a dog," she answered in lieu of Ethan's satisfied grin, which made her distinctly uncomfortable. It didn't take much to figure out what her sister might be thinking, and probably was. "A *guard* dog."

"Cool," Ginger said again. "What's his name? Can we introduce him to the others?"

Glory sighed. "His name is Bruno and yes, that's the general idea."

"*Bruno?* That sounds like a bulldog or mastiff or something, not a German shepherd."

Ethan cracked up. "That's exactly what Glory said."

He turned to her with that wry purse of his lips. "See? You and your sister are more alike than you realize."

Ginger appeared to appreciate Ethan's comment, if her beaming face was any indication. Glory wasn't so sure it was a compliment.

Why would Ginger want to be like *her?* Given the choice...

"Well, what are we waiting for?" Ethan asked, eager and impatient. "Bring on the kids."

"Don't you think—" Glory began, but Ginger cut her off. "I'll go get the kids and sweep by the computer room. Glory, you holler at the gals in the den."

She sighed. This was obviously going to happen with or without her. She might as well do as Ginger said. At least then she'd have a moment to warn the ladies what they were getting into.

Warning appeared not to apply when she mentioned the fact that Ethan was bringing in a dog for everyone to meet, a possible new watchdog.

She hadn't seen such enthusiasm in the place since the day the computers arrived. It was almost a stampede as some women dashed for the front hall, while others rushed to the children's quarters to round up any stray kids.

Glory followed distractedly behind the chattering group of ladies, lost in her own thoughts. She wished she could run the other way and not face this moment with Ethan.

By the time she reached the front room, Bruno was completely surrounded by two-dozen clamoring people of all sizes and ages. Even the other shelter workers were joining in the fray. Little

Meggie toddled around right in the center of the mob, with Bruno flanking her faithfully.

The dog didn't seem to mind the commotion at all. In fact, it appeared he was quite happy. His tail wagged enthusiastically as he turned every which direction, licking whatever child's hand or cheek was closest.

This was precisely the kind of sanitary issues she'd been talking about, among others, she thought, feeling self-justified even if the truth was she loved dogs and didn't really consider them unhealthy.

Besides, she doubted any words of warning, especially from her, would be heard above this din. She'd heard less racket at major league baseball games.

Another big score for Ethan Wheeler, and three cheers for the same.

She realized how unkind her thoughts were, and prayed forgiveness for them. Ethan was the best man she'd ever known, yet she directed her anger at him as if he were the root of the problem.

The worst part was, he wasn't. The dog wasn't even the real issue. Bruno wasn't why she was so cross and snippy this morning.

With a shake of her head, she backed away,

slipping away to her office where she could be alone and regain her equilibrium.

Sighing, she propped her hands behind her head and leaned back in her chair, squeezing her eyes closed until she could see sparkling lights on the back of her eyelids.

This was going to be one very long day. And it didn't look as if it was going to stop any time soon.

She'd woken up this morning with nothing but wonderful, giddy thoughts about the evening she and Ethan had shared.

The way it felt to see sweet Meggie napping on her floor, content as if she were in her own little crib.

The way Ethan made himself at home, making his way around her house as if it were his own.

Even the way that silly dog had curled up around the hearth and looked for all the world like the cherished family pet.

She chuckled at the memories. Last night wasn't something she'd forget easily.

Ever.

Ethan's kiss had been the highlight of an evening of highlights. There weren't words to express the fantastical discoveries she'd made in the brushing of their lips, the sharing of their combined breath, the way her heartbeat had matched his pace for pace.

She'd not known such bliss existed; certainly not here on earth. To find a place where there was, for as long as it lasted, peace, pleasure and contentment, with the added advantage of the complete repression of anything bad.

No past or future; only the moment at hand. A magnificent combination of elements, if ever there was one.

But of course that had ended when Ethan walked out her front door with Bruno and Meggie in tow. The house was once again empty and sterile.

Like her heart, she supposed.

Last night had been wonderful—which was exactly why it couldn't happen again.

She would simply have to tell Ethan it had been a mistake. She knew he wouldn't want to hear it, but he certainly couldn't deny it.

They were as different as night and day.

More to the point, they were working together at Angel's Wings.

She'd completely panicked this morning when she and Ethan had arrived at the shelter at the same time. All she could think about was that it might look to others as if they'd come together.

It probably had, though her sister hadn't seemed terribly surprised or shocked. If Ginger knew things had changed, she hadn't said a word.

But if she unintentionally hurt anyone....

She couldn't do her job as the shelter director if she was constantly worried about what other people were thinking about her and Ethan, wondering if they were spending their free time together. Wondering how their relationship was progressing.

Relationship? When had it become a relationship?

It *wasn't*.

She would just have to make Ethan see why what happened last night couldn't happen again. Not if they were going to keep working with each other, as she sincerely hoped they would.

Ethan got nothing out of his time at Angel's Wings beyond God's blessing and the satisfaction of a job well done. Yet he'd done far more than he'd originally planned, drawn in by a combination of his goodness and kindness, and of the guilt he bore from his relationship with his cousin.

Neither of them had known at the time that the computers had been just the beginning.

Lately, he and Meggie were practically daily

fixtures here, with no sign of leaving. Everyone—
and she meant *everyone*—knew and loved them.

And she loved them most of all.

She was still musing on the subject when Ginger knocked softly at her door.

"Everything okay, sis?"

Glory did her best to smile. "Of course. Why
would you think anything was wrong?"

Ginger's blue eyes glowed with amusement and
concern. "C'mon, Glory. This is me you're talking to."

She shook a finger under Glory's nose.
"Maybe no one else noticed, but you lit out of
the hall like your tail was on fire. Spill the beans,
sis. What's the story?"

Glory scowled, then realized she was better off
fading her expression to feigned innocence.
"There is no story."

"Right."

Okay, so she wasn't buying it. Heaven knew
her sister wouldn't give up, not when she smelled
a *story*. Glory banked herself for the inevitable
attack.

Ginger obliged her with a wry smile. "You
walk in looking like you're about ready to jump
out of your skin. You won't even glance at Ethan
or me, never mind make eye contact."

Glory looked away, and Ginger snorted merrily. "I'm slow, but not stupid. There's definitely a story. And it is *definitely* a story I want to hear."

Her mind raced with what she might say. Anything except the truth—that Ethan had kissed her and she was wigging out, as the young people at the shelter would call it.

Ginger tapped her chin thoughtfully. "Is it the dog? Are you mad at Ethan because of Bruno?"

"I'm not mad at Ethan," Glory snapped, annoyed that she sounded annoyed.

Ginger threw her arms up and took a mock step backward. "Whoa. So that's the way the wind blows. Or should I say hurricane?"

"What are you talking about?"

"Ethan." Ginger hovered over her, not allowing Glory to break eye contact. Sweat beaded on her forehead and the back of her neck. Was this what the Inquisition had been like?

"Ethan kissed me."

Glory smacked a hand over her mouth, but it was too late. The damage was done.

Oh, her big mouth!

Mortified, she swung her chair around so she wouldn't have to see the smug, I-told-you-so look in Ginger's eyes. She gritted her teeth, preparing

herself for the lecture her sister was sure to give—
if she ever stopped laughing.

Except she wasn't laughing—not even a telltale
chuckle.

Instead, a few silent moments after Glory's ap-
palling revelation, she felt her chair being pulled
slowly and firmly back around.

She tensed, then relaxed at the concerned expression on her sister's face. No hint of teasing,
no amusement twinkling in her eyes. Glory's
throat tightened in response.

Ginger knelt by her sister, reaching a hand to
clasp Glory's two in her lap. She was smiling, but
it was a kind smile, not smug at all.

Glory couldn't have been more surprised at her
sister's kindness. Not that Ginger wasn't a kind
woman—she was, and Glory had seen it many
times at the shelter and elsewhere.

But the two of them shared a unique relationship, with Ginger playing the ever irascible little
sister.

Since they'd been small, she'd been an incur-
able tease, always looking for something to tor-
ment Glory about. And naturally, over time, Glory
had become defensive toward Ginger's constant
prodding and joking.

The Glory-Ginger paradox defined their relationship now, and as backward as it seemed, Glory was lost without it.

"Glory?" Ginger queried softly, breaking into her thoughts. "Sweetheart? I don't want to pry."

Glory shot her a look that clearly revealed her disbelief.

"Really, Glory. Cross my heart. I *don't* want to pry."

"Hammer it out of me, then," Glory returned, unable to stop herself from bantering.

Ginger grinned, then put her hands flat under her chin and batted her eyelashes. "Who, me? I'm just confused. There's a very important piece missing from this puzzle of yours."

Her catty grin revealed her true intentions. "Why is Ethan kissing you a problem?"

In any other situation, Glory would have suspected Ginger's motives. But now, for some reason, she believed Ginger was sincere, despite the wicked grin. And she definitely needed someone she could share her dilemma with, someone who might be able to give her some much needed advice.

"It was wonderful," she confided in a whisper. "*He* is wonderful."

Ginger chuckled. "I'm not seeing the problem here, Glory. You like him. He obviously likes you. This has the makings of happily-ever-after, if you ask me, which you didn't.''

"Oh, Ginger. That's exactly it. There can't *be* a happily-ever-after.''

Ginger's eyebrows hit her hairline, and she shook her head in disbelief. ''At the risk of repeating myself, I don't see the problem.''

"Isn't it obvious?''

She grinned. ''*Obviously* not.''

"I can't run the shelter if I'm carrying on with Ethan.''

"Glory, having a relationship with a man is hardly carrying on with him.''

"You know what I mean.''

Ginger sighed loudly. ''Yes, I know exactly what you mean. You're embarrassed. As simple as that. Or, in my dear sister's case, as impossible as that.''

"Impossible. Thanks a lot, sis.''

Glory stood so suddenly her chair spun on its casters. ''Look, I know you're trying to be helpful. I do. But right now I need to be alone.'' She gestured toward the door to her office.

"Well, I'm not leaving,'' said Ginger stubbornly, crossing her arms for emphasis.

"Fine,'' Glory snapped back. ''Then I am.''

She followed her words with the deed itself,

stomping out of her own office to find a place to be alone. If this wasn't the ultimate stain on her dignity, she didn't know what was.

Or maybe—probably—the worst was yet to come.

Ethan.

Part of her regretted her churlish behavior toward her sister. She knew Ginger was only acting out of the goodness of her heart, even if she completely misunderstood the situation, and more to the point, misunderstood how Glory felt.

She sighed deeply, feeling a deep, almost physical heaviness within her chest, a heaviness that pulled her spirits down as well. It seemed she was ever asking God for forgiveness for her mouth getting the best of her.

Her attitude wasn't exactly without fault, either. She could at least admit that.

It was just that she always panicked. And when she panicked, her brain shut off and her mouth ran away with her.

She might appear calm, cool and collected to the outside world, but on the inside, she was a quivering mess. Indecisive. Insecure.

Maybe that's why she tried so hard *not* to react emotionally at the shelter, no matter what the crisis or catastrophe. What she'd just displayed with

Ginger—that open, emotional woman—was nothing less than weakness, in her book.

And she couldn't afford weakness. The shelter women and children depended on her strength.

Reminded of her God-given obligations, she stopped barreling down the hallway, leaned her arm against the wall, and squeezed her eyes closed.

Lord God, may I find strength in You, that I might be strong for those in my care. I know I've failed them, Lord. Give me renewed strength of thought, mind and spirit. I won't let You down again.

Fortified by her internal monologue and prayer, she toyed with the idea of going back to the front room and welcoming the erstwhile and very hairy Bruno into the family, but upon turning into a kitchen full of dirty dishes, decided not to return. At least not yet.

A few more minutes alone wouldn't hurt. Ginger wouldn't follow her, not with her tongue-lashing so fresh. No one would find her here.

A feeling of internal peace encompassed her, now that she had her sights set back on the Lord and on the shelter, and had her decisions quite firmly and resolutely made.

She knew her spirit wouldn't stay serene for long, and she wanted to savor it while it lasted.

Donning an apron, she filled a sink with suds and began absently scrubbing away, her mind going over the many details she'd been neglecting while her head had been in the clouds with Ethan—*no*. She'd better not actually think about him by name, at least not for a while.

Until her heart got used to being alone.

Nonsense. She'd been alone before, and it hadn't mattered a bit. What made her situation now so very different?

It suddenly felt very empty in the vacant and echoing kitchen. The clang of the silverware she set in another sink to rinse suddenly sounded altogether too loud.

Deciding she'd quit after this one sink of dishes, she began humming a hymn, something to listen to besides the quiet. Before long, she was lost in the joy of praising God. She wasn't aware of her surroundings anymore, at least until she felt a gentle elbow nudge her in the ribs.

"Hey, gorgeous. We've got to stop meeting here like this. What would the help think?"

Chapter Thirteen

❧

"**E**than!" She hoped she didn't sound as surprised and stunned as she felt, but even she could hear that her voice was squeaking.

"None other," he said with his usual purse-lipped, crooked grin. "Were you expecting some other devastatingly handsome man?"

"No, of course not. I mean..." She clamped her mouth shut.

She looked up to see he'd already slung a towel over his shoulder and was drying a dinner plate. Her heart did a double take, as it always did, at the magnificent man beside her.

She was making a muddle of this, and she hadn't even started. She'd expected to be able to have the upper hand in her conversation with Ethan—selecting the time and place, at the very least.

This was neither the time nor the place, yet she couldn't just go on pretending nothing was bothering her, or that nothing had changed.

She owed Ethan the truth. He was a good man, and he deserved so much more.

"Hey, not a problem, gorgeous. You don't have to explain anything to me. Let's just say I noticed that you disappeared as soon as we got here. And when you didn't come back after a while..."

He cleared his throat. "I hope Bruno didn't run you off."

"No. I've been giving it some thought, and I believe you're right about a watchdog being a good idea for the shelter. Bruno stays if I have anything to say about it. A conference call to the board should seal the deal."

Feeling a little bit more in her element, she gambled making eye contact with him. "Do I need to go down to the kennel for the paperwork, or can you bring it to me? I probably need to go there, right? So they can check out the potential owner, and all that. That's just as well—I can sign us up for that training you were talking about last night.''

His eyebrows hit the ceiling, but she ignored his expression and continued.

"They'll be five of us—myself, Ginger, and three others," she continued, counting on her fingers. "Oh, and you, of course. Please feel free to add your own name if you'd like."

Ethan opened his mouth. She didn't know if it was a signal that he wanted to speak, or shock that she was rambling, but she just couldn't stop herself from talking.

"The first available date would be best. If we're going to do this thing, we may as well get on it and do it right."

Finally, to even her own astonishment, she closed her mouth.

The ensuing silence was a mockery of her extraordinary speech.

Ethan looked pleased, but still very stunned. "Whoa, lady, you never stop astonishing me. Tell me, when we've been together for twenty years, will you still spring stuff like this on me?"

She grimaced. Brace yourself, Ethan Wheeler, because I haven't even started.

"I prayed about it," she admitted in a mumble.

"Thank You, God," Ethan chimed in immediately and cheerfully.

Glory felt as if she would choke. "Please don't tease about God."

He shook his head fervently. "I'm not. I do thank God. Especially for you."

He was serious. Completely, absolutely serious. Over her, of all things.

Serious about God. The man who'd made light of the God of Angel's Wings. He'd obviously found that God here.

She wanted to cry with happiness and laugh in bitterness, all at the same time.

The knowledge that she would hurt him ached to the point of physical pain in the general area of her heart.

And she would hurt him. She'd known that even before his last words.

No man would like hearing what she would be forced to tell him, and Ethan was more kind and sensitive than most. And if he cared for her in more than just a casual way....

But surely after she'd explained, after he'd had a chance to think about it, he'd see the rightness of her convictions.

Perhaps he'd *already* thought about it. Ethan was an irredeemable flirt.

Besides, she rationalized, it wasn't like they wouldn't see each other at the shelter. That was the whole point, wasn't it—they had to *work* together at the shelter nearly every day?

Ethan hooted a laugh that made Glory stiffen and swing her gaze to him. He looked amused.

Sometimes that joyful twinkle in his eye drove her crazy, especially now. And at the moment, she'd rather wipe the characteristic purse in his lips—the one that lingered just short of a smirk—right off the man's happy face.

"Is something funny? My glasses are on crooked? What?"

"I asked you a question, and you didn't answer." He grinned incorrigibly. "Thus, my—ahem—laughter."

"Come again?" The knots in her stomach and shoulders were quickly turning into rocks. Why, oh why did Ethan's presence have to turn her inside out? Where was all her self-control?

"My question," he said, broadening the word dramatically in lawyerlike fashion, "was why on earth would I find you washing dishes on a busy Saturday? I mean, really. It's not like there aren't procedures for this sort of thing."

As tense as she was, feeling like a cannon about ready to go off, she couldn't help but chuckle, despite knowing laughter was a sure step down the hard road to tears. He was talking about their chore poster, which laid out the duties of the residents.

As Ethan had pointed out earlier, every new person she introduced to the shelter was a potential danger, so the women and teenagers mostly cared for the large household themselves.

Actually, Glory had found cleaning to be an excellent means to building back a battered woman's self-esteem. It was reassuring somehow, to take a messy room and make it neat and clean.

But that was hardly the point right now. Ethan was still talking, and she wasn't paying attention.

"So I asked myself," he said, rubbing his hands on the towel at his shoulder and turning toward her, leaning his right hip on the counter. "What would a woman like you be doing in a place like this?"

Only Ethan.

"At first I thought you just wanted to get away from Bruno, of course, but you've just—and quite eloquently, I might add—explained that Bruno is not your problem."

He frowned and squinted at her. "So what *is* your problem?"

He made the question sound so inflammatory

that someone coming into the kitchen at the moment would have thought they were having a fight. Glory knew better. Ethan was just being...well, *Ethan*.

Once again, she reaffirmed her commitment to follow through with what must be. What if one of the more needful shelter women barged in on her shelter director having a "fight" with one of the shelter's most adamant supporters?

She sighed aloud. It was time.

"Ethan," she began, but paused, thinking through her words carefully. "You, um—might have noticed I sort of, well, *ignored* you when we came in to the shelter together this morning."

Ethan cocked his head and tried to capture Glory's gaze. He'd heard her sudden change in tone, or maybe her serious tenor had been there all along and he'd just now noticed it.

Either way, something serious was going down.

He wanted to reach out to Glory, to hold her and reassure her against whatever was ailing her, but he knew better than to do that. She had her pride, and he wasn't about to step on it.

Not that his arms wouldn't be readily available when the time came, as he knew it would—the time when she was ready to come to him and accept what he offered.

Which, for a matter of record, was his whole blooming heart.

"Yes. As I said earlier, I noticed your posthaste disappearance from the front hallway when we first arrived."

"Exactly," she said in a husky whisper.

He shrugged. "I just thought Bruno—"

"It's *not* Bruno," she shouted, then clapped a hand over her mouth and dashed a look at each of the doors. Her expression was mortified, as if she expected to see someone leaning on the door frame watching her.

Apparently satisfied they were alone in the room, she narrowed her gaze on him and continued in a hiss. "It's not the stupid, silly mutt."

"I think we've established that point," he commented with a wry purse of his lips. "But you still haven't told me what's wrong."

She sighed, her hands tightly clasped in front of her. "Nothing's wrong, exactly. At least, that's not the word I'd use."

She paused and took a deep gulp of air. Ethan was beginning to get worried. Glory was usually tied up in a twist about something, but this seemed severe even for her.

"So nothing's wrong and we're doing dishes

together. Works for me.'' He grinned and stuck
his hands in the suds.''

Glory's hand on his arm brought him up short.
''You don't always have to be doing something
for me—for us, Ethan, though the goodness of
your heart flows all the way through Angel's
Wings.''

Ethan frowned; the deep guilt he'd been living
with for so long reapplied itself with a vengeance
to his chest and shoulders. ''I could never, *ever*
do enough for Angel's Wings. Not if I worked
here every day of my life.''

Glory was the only one he'd ever told of the
situation with Sabrina. She alone would understand his desire to make amends, to somehow
erase the stain of his guilt on the death of his
cousin.

Still, he realized how abrasive his words
sounded, and he backed off. ''And as for doing
enough for you, my dear, it would be my very
great pleasure to be allowed to keep doing things
for you.''

To his frustration, Glory turned away from him
and wrapped her arms around herself in what
looked like a self-comforting gesture.

Why couldn't she find comfort in *his* arms?

''Ethan, we've got to stop seeing each other.''

His breath rushed suddenly from his lungs, as if he'd been sucker punched in the ribs with no warning. As a matter of fact, that was *exactly* how he felt at the moment.

Shoving his fingers through his thick hair, he struggled to recover from the shock. He sucked in a big breath, ignoring the choking sensation that ensued when the air met his closed throat. Pressing his lips together, he tried to think through Glory's reasoning, to come up with why she'd made such an outrageous statement in the first place.

Why hadn't he seen this coming? Glory always went into a tizzy when situations went beyond her immediate control. It was one of the traits he adored about her, the crazy woman.

Guess that made him a little bit crazy, too. Crazy in love, that was.

"Is that all that's bothering you?" he asked lightly.

"What?" Shocked didn't begin to describe the high-pitched sound of her voice.

He grinned. He liked throwing her off balance a bit just to see her reaction. This time, it was a diversionary tactic—something to keep him in the game while he struggled to figure out what she was really saying.

He continued with a forced grin. "It's obviously a problem—that we're seeing each other, I mean."

Her eyes were dual round saucers, so he kept it up, pushed harder.

"Like you said," he reminded her. "But there's a simple solution, really."

"Really?" Now she sounded a little relieved and a lot bewildered.

"Really."

He knew she wanted him to explain, so of course he paused thoughtfully. "One of us will have to wear a blindfold."

He raced on, presumably oblivious to the strangled sound she made in her throat. "I volunteer, of course. The manly thing to do, don't you think?"

For all his efforts, he was rewarded by another strangled sound. He wondered drolly if he ought not perform the Heimlich maneuver on her.

His grin widened, for real this time. "Perhaps we ought to have it be ladies first? Oh, I know! We'll split the effort right down the middle. Half-and-half. Fifty-fifty."

He pulled out a quarter from his pocket and tossed it in the air. "Should we flip to see who goes first? Or do you prefer rock, paper, scissors?''

Her face had turned an alarming shade of red, and he realized belatedly that he'd gone too far, pushed her beyond her limit.

She apparently agreed with his assessment, because the next moment she pegged him in the chest with a very wet washcloth and whirled around, heading toward the nearest exit.

He went after her, grabbing her by the elbow, which she quickly shirked off. She didn't turn to face him, but she didn't leave, either, to his relief.

"Look…that was a really lousy thing I said to you back there. I'm—"

"Incorrigible," Glory snapped, turning around. Tears poured from her eyes, but other than that one word, she was completely silent.

He flashed her his best grin. "I was going to say sorry."

A wavering smile lit her face. "Yes. That, too."

"Why do I think you're using the second dictionary definition of the word?"

He raised his voice an octave to imitate Glory. "Ethan Wheeler, you're the *sorriest* individual I've ever met in my life."

She chuckled.

Feeling as if they'd regained their sense of equilibrium, he took her hand and drew her back into the kitchen, into a quiet corner where she could pull up a chair if she wanted to, where she'd feel safe, and where prying eyes might not see them.

It was time to get to the bottom of this situation once and for all.

Chapter Fourteen

Glory allowed him to pull her with him into the far corner of the kitchen, though she was suddenly quite dubious about talking to him. She'd realized the error in blurting out her feelings just after they left her mouth.

Of course Ethan would want to hash it out here and now, before God and everyone. A public kitchen was neither the time nor the place for such an effort. They risked much of a possibility of running into other people.

In all likelihood, Ginger would come looking for her after a while, though if she realized Ethan was missing as well, she'd probably drag her feet getting here.

As usual, Ethan asserted himself in such a joyful, carefree way that she couldn't help but give in to him.

It annoyed her that he knew the power of his smile, and used it to his advantage. She knew she should be angry with him.

She often was, but it never lasted long.

The crazy thing was, she was even more in love with Ethan for all his antics. She'd balked because she was afraid she'd blurt out that she loved him and would have to leave the shelter to fend for itself.

He'd thought she was angry, of course. She was, but not at him. She was mad at herself, for her lack of faith and courage in following her convictions. Mad about being a wimp of the first degree.

It didn't matter what her feelings dictated where Ethan was concerned. She had to look to the best interest of the shelter.

She'd told herself the same thing a thousand times, and it still didn't ring true in her heart. At the moment, all she wanted to do was throw herself in Ethan's arms and beg him to kiss her just the way he had last evening.

"Do you want to sit?" He shoved his fingers through the tips of his hair, leaving them at whichever angle they drew. This was as edgy as she'd ever seen him. Even his smile looked forced.

She looked away. She'd never get through this if she had to look him in the eye.

"What happened last night," she began, then paused. "Not that it wasn't, uh, wonderful. It...was."

Her speech was as choppy as her thoughts. She sat down, trying to relax and gather herself together for her next round.

Ethan leaned over and planted a gentle kiss on her forehead, his hand brushing lightly across her hair. "I thought it was, uh—wonderful, too," he whispered, close enough to her ear for her to feel the warmth of his breath, and to hear the trademark chuckle that followed his statement.

"Nevertheless," she continued determinedly, "it can't happen again."

He cocked his head, then shook it adamantly. "Glory, you—"

"*I* have thought over the implications of last night," she interrupted.

"You think I haven't been thinking about it? C'mon, Glory, all I've been thinking about since last night is *last night*."

She sighed. He was being obtuse, and they both knew it. Why couldn't he just once give it a rest?

"It would not be in our best interests to continue our personal relationship in light of our relationship at the shelter here."

She could see he was struggling to keep his jaw from dropping at her outrageous statement.

"And that would be why?"

"These women are my responsibility, Ethan, and I can't afford to—I *mustn't*—let anything or anyone get in the way of that duty."

"No one's asking you to—"

"I know no one is asking. No one would. That's why I have to take it on myself to do what's right. As much as I love when we're together, I cannot forgive myself for not being there—*here*, at the shelter—when I'm needed.

"I sincerely hope you'll recognize your magnificent contribution to Angel's Wings. You have quite literally changed the atmosphere around here, and I hope you'll want to continue your work. We'll simply have to make ours a platonic, business relationship."

Ethan was grinding his teeth so hard his jaw ached from the effort. If she'd let him get a word in edgewise, let him finish a sentence, maybe they could work this out. But as long as she continued to speak for him, they'd get nowhere.

He shook his head and tried again. "But I'm not—"

"Distracting? Yes, actually you are."

"Okay, that's it," he announced sternly, knowing she wouldn't know what to do with such a statement.

He knew he was right when silence ensued. Joy to his ears.

Gripping her firmly by the shoulders, he raised her to her feet.

"*Fatal Distraction,* indeed." He snorted and bent to remove her glasses, placing them on a nearby counter.

"The only distraction here, Glory, is you. You and your ideas of what the shelter requires of you. Open your eyes, gorgeous. Life goes on whether you're there or not.

"God didn't ask you to make such an outrageous commitment, and neither did the board of directors or the women themselves. They recognize even when you can't that you can't be refreshed to serve them if you never get any downtime yourself.

"It's a simple equation. You, me, Meggie and God. You can serve Christ better by being *with* me than without me. And you do the same for me—make me a better man than I could be alone. Can't you see that?"

When she tried to turn away from him, he slid his hands up to gently grasp her jaw. "Can't you?"

Tears rolled down her cheeks and over the backs of his hands. He squeezed his eyes shut, knowing the answer before it came.

"No, Ethan. I can't see it that way. I've tried, but I can't."

He heard the agony in her voice, but he couldn't find it in his heart to find sympathy for a woman who was throwing both their happy futures away.

He pulled her closer. She'd look him in the eyes this one last time.

"I have my limits, too, Glory. If I leave today without you, I won't be back to Angel's Wings."

She jolted in his arms, but he wouldn't let her go.

He closed his lips over hers, not really knowing why. But instead of the hard, passionate kiss he'd intended, he kissed her softly, tenderly.

It was his goodbye kiss, as well as hers. He might as well make it the best it could be.

A slam and a shout intruded, and they jumped

apart like dual sparks as Stephen dashed toward them. "Miss Glory! Mr. Ethan! Hurry!"

Ethan took his model from Glory, who casually slid her hands across her tousled hair and squared her shoulders.

He didn't miss the shaded look she flashed at him. He wasn't really good at having to be told I told you so.

The boy was out of breath and shifting from foot to foot. He was obviously distressed, but he'd stopped dead when he'd reached them. No doubt from seeing the two of them kissing.

"What's up, Steve-o?"

Ethan asked the question, but Stephen directed the answer to Glory. "Dad's here, Miss Glory."

Glory's arm was around Stephen in a heartbeat. "Are you telling me you've seen your father here? At the shelter?"

The young man nodded vigorously, and then dashed a wayward tear away with the back of a dirty hand. Judging from his clothes, he'd been outside playing football with the other boys.

Ethan saw Glory's jaw tense, but other than that, she showed no sign of fear or dismay, only a calm concern. At that moment, Ethan was glad she was so strong, and saw just what that tough veneer meant to her, and to the shelter residents.

"Son, I want you to tell me exactly where you think your father is at this moment, and your mother, as well. Take your time. I need an educated guess."

The boy nodded. "When I left, Dad was talking to Mom in the main hallway."

"Okay. I want you to go back to your room and stay there, all right? I'll let you know when it's safe to come out."

Glory patted the boy on the shoulder, a gesture Ethan suspected the boy wouldn't have allowed from her four months ago when they'd first arrived at Angel's Wings.

Stephen merely nodded, eyes wide.

"It'll be fine, Stephen. You'll see."

As Stephen went the back way to find his room, Ethan's gaze rose to Glory's. "What about his sister? Will Mary be okay?"

Glory nodded grimly. "She's probably in the children's dayroom. Her teacher will have to be alerted, though."

Ethan reached his hand to Glory, and to his relief, she accepted and returned the gesture. "I'll slip through the back way and make sure the little ones are safely tucked away, then meet you in the hallway."

She nodded again. "Thank you," she whispered coarsely.

He pursed his lips and turned toward the back door.

"Ethan?"

He spun around, soaking in Glory's frightened but determined gaze. "Yes?"

She smiled softly. "Pray hard."

Chapter Fifteen

❧

"Now, look, everyone," Mark said as he stood virtually surrounded by staff and Lena's anxious friends. He gestured persuasively with his hands.

On the other end of the hallway, stood Lena, looking small and mussed, her own arms wrapped around herself protectively.

"No harm meant," Mark insisted. "I only want to see my wife."

Glory's throat was so tight she thought she might choke. The only difference between this Lena and the one who'd come crawling into Angel's Wings four months ago was the fire of determination blazing from her gaze.

But would that be enough?

"Go home, Mark," Lena said softly, but firmly. "You know you have a restraining order out on you."

"Yeah, I know," he said, his voice at once soft and hard. He looked like a well-off businessman in his weekend wear—khaki slacks, grass-green polo shirt with the collar cocked up. A golf-yellow cardigan. Penny loafers. Well-tanned, blond and muscular.

Typical husband. Typical abuser.

"Baby, I've missed you," he half whined, half coaxed.

Lena dropped her head and didn't answer.

"I love you." He reached out to her and took a step forward, but the group around him squeezed against his progress. "You know I do.

"Come on, baby. I just want to talk to you." His gaze made a sweep of the company, lingering on Glory with narrowed eyes. She wondered how he knew, but he did.

Her skin burned. The face-off with the shelter's director was an inevitable part of what he was doing, breaking in like this. He had to know that, too.

"So talk," Lena said roughly. Her hands shook as she stood to her full height.

Mark shifted and waved his hand. "I can't talk here. Not with all these people around."

He swept a glance in Glory's direction and grinned like a cat, then took another step toward Lena.

And another.

Glory felt as if she were watching a movie in slow motion. She knew she needed to act, to step in and stop whatever was happening, yet her feet felt frozen to the floor.

She'd never felt so alone. If ever she needed help, it was now.

Where was Ethan? How long could it take to check the dayroom? Major fireworks were about to explode, and he wasn't here to help.

She needed him. Desperately.

"I know I did wrong, Lena. Give me some credit. I made a mistake. But I've changed. I swear it. I'll never touch you again. I'll make it up to you, baby, you know I will. Please. Just let me talk to you for a minute."

Lena wavered at his pleading drawl, then lifted her face, tears streaming down her cheeks.

"Ten years of marriage, Lena. You want to just throw it all away? Think of the good times we had, you and me."

Oh, he was smooth. Every word coming out of his mouth was a coy mixture of truth and fancy.

Glory knew she should be screaming, drowning out the words that made a woman turn and trust a man who could not be trusted.

"Lena?" Mark continued. "Just a few minutes. We can stay here. What harm could it do?"

To Glory's horror, Lena nodded. "Only a minute, though."

Glory had panicked, and now it was too late. What Ethan said had been right. She couldn't do it alone.

Still, she stepped forward. If Lena wanted to meet with Mark, she couldn't stop her; but she could set the parameters of the meet.

"Mark, I'm Glory Weston, the shelter director."

Mark nodded but didn't look at her. His gaze was wholly focused on Lena, and the look he gave her had Glory in chills.

"You have five minutes. I'll escort you to a hallway where you may walk and talk," she continued, thinking of the hallway on the farthest side of the shelter from the children's dayroom and Lena's living quarters.

Glory quickly gave orders to her staff, then showed the two down the hallway. She stepped out of sight, but didn't leave. She had no idea how she might help by hovering around, but she couldn't just leave Lena here.

She could hear them talking softly, him persuading, her disagreeing. Nothing to be concerned about. Yet.

Which was why she bowed her head in prayer.

One moment. One single moment was all it took to send a batterer into a violent rage, and Mark had proven himself persistent. Whatever he wanted, she doubted he'd leave before he got it.

Suddenly she felt something wet and sticky lick her ear. *Bruno!*

She'd forgotten about the dog until now. A serious-faced Ginger had him by the lead.

"I thought he might help," she whispered. "He didn't come with instructions on his collar, though. Do you know how to command him?"

Glory shook her head. They'd have to figure it out. A *guard* dog. Surely Bruno would help if the situation between Mark and Lena got out of hand.

"The police are here," Ginger continued. "I'm keeping everyone back."

Glory nodded, wanting to hug her sister tight and knowing now was not the time. "Keep them back," she agreed. If Mark saw police uniforms, he'd certainly panic.

When Ginger withdrew, Glory clung to the German shepherd like a lifeline, the answer to her prayers. And somehow, cuddled in his fur, the danger of the situation seemed less imminent than it had earlier.

Voices had risen, so she told the dog to stay and hoped he wouldn't make any noise. Creeping on all fours, she peered around the corner.

Mark had Lena pinned against a wall, dangling her nearly off the floor by her neck. She was struggling and kicking madly, but he just laughed.

"Let her go." Glory launched to her feet and barreled down the hallway to stand and face Mark off. *"Now."*

Mark immediately released Lena, who backed away slowly, delicately holding her neck. "Yeah, you're right. Okay. I got a little upset. But we were talking about my kids, okay?"

"Okay," Glory agreed, keeping her voice calm and even. The best thing to do was not to rile him any further. Just get him to agree to leave.

Somehow.

Her mind was a blank. Again. And time was ticking away Lena's chances of getting away clean.

"Aw, everyone's having a party and I wasn't

invited. I have to say, I'm devastated. After all these years being neighbors...."

Ethan waltzed into the hallway from the opposite end, looking for all the world as if he *was* going to a backyard barbecue. He sauntered up with a cavalier attitude, hands casually tucked into his pockets, whistling under his breath.

But when his gaze met hers, she knew he was totally serious. He'd obviously taken stock of the situation and was moving in according to some kind of plan.

At least, she hoped he had some kind of plan.

"Hot dogs, anyone?"

She could see where he was walking—covering the distance between Mark and Lena.

No one breathed. Mark looked around desperately. Lena looked horrified, frozen to the spot.

"No? Well, then, I guess it's time for everyone to leave." He looked straight at Mark.

Mark reached for Lena in such a lightning-quick motion that she was wrapped in his arms faster than anyone could do anything about, least of all Glory.

"I don't think so, buddy," Mark replied in his gravelly voice. "My *wife* and I aren't finished talking yet. And it sure isn't any of your business."

Ethan pursed his lips in the way he had that looked almost like a low, irritating smirk. She didn't think Mark needed to be egged on, but she didn't know how to communicate with Ethan short of speaking out loud, which would be fruitless.

Slowly, steadily, he moved toward Mark.

Glory held her breath.

"Is that a fact?" Ethan drawled, nearly mimicking Mark's voice.

"That's a *fact*." Surely Ethan couldn't miss that hard edge.

"Well, the way I look at it, Lena and me are good friends. And as a friend, I have the obligation to protect her from nozzles like you."

Where the handgun came from Ethan couldn't have said. He'd slid a glance at Glory, and when he'd turned back, the gun was there, being waved around by nothing short of a madman.

Slowly and deliberately, making firm, hard eye contact with Ethan, Mark pointed the gun at Lena's forehead and put pressure on the trigger.

"I don't want *you*," he barked huskily into Lena's hair. He tightened his grip and nearly pulled her off the floor with the force of his clutch.

"Let her go, Mark," Glory said smoothly.

"You can't get what you want this way. Just let Lena go. Give her to me. Then we can all talk when everyone has regained their composure."

She was very good at negotiating, with her soft, persuasive tone, but Mark was obviously not phased by it as Ethan was.

Mark jerked Lena around, trying to take both Glory and Ethan into his gaze. "I didn't come here to talk. I didn't come for this little tramp, either."

A wide-eyed Lena remained frozen with the gun pointed at her forehead.

Ethan slid sideways so he and Glory were facing each other across the hallway, and thus making it impossible for Mark to keep them both well in view. He watched the gun with care, and kept a close eye on Glory.

A couple of times, she gestured faintly toward the hallway and tried to tell him something with her lips, but even through his rushing adrenaline, he couldn't understand her charade.

Mark swung Lena around like a rag doll. Ethan could see the blue marks forming on her arms and neck. It was all he could do to keep a lid on his anger. Especially with Mark's continued rambling, which grated against everything Ethan stood for.

God, country and family. None of these meant anything to Mark, not if his constant, slurred cursing had anything to say about it. Mark was angry and frustrated, and at the moment, he was in control of the situation.

Ethan's blood screamed for action, but he knew he'd be foolish to act without thinking and planning. He would *not* put Glory or Lena into further danger by his actions, yet paradoxically he *needed* to act to get the ladies out of danger.

"I don't care about the court order, and I don't care about the divorce." Mark waved the gun around like a baton, using it to make his points.

Then his eye and his gun landed on Glory, and Ethan knew he had to gain control of the situation now.

He was here to save Lena, and he would. But his heart stopped beating altogether at the thought of losing Glory, especially to some crazy man with a gun, ready to unload on the woman Ethan loved.

No way. It wasn't going to happen. It *wasn't* going to happen.

Mark swiveled on his feet, almost as if he were drunk, though his gun remained firmly pointed toward Glory.

"I want my son, and I want him now," Mark demanded. "Man's got a right to his son."

"We can talk about it," Glory coaxed. "Just put down the gun."

Instead of following Glory's suggestion, he pressed his lips together and aimed the pistol directly at Glory's head.

Sweat poured down his face, dampening his golf clothes. "The way I figure it, if I shoot one of you, I'll get what I want. *Stephen.*"

Glory and Lena gasped simultaneously—not at being named as prospective victims, but at the idea of Stephen being sent away with Mark. And surely they were also thinking about little Mary in the dayroom.

Think, Ethan commanded himself, wiping sweat from his own forehead. *Think!*

Mark was caught like a wild dog in a corner, and he would use any means at his disposal to get what he wanted. He was also clearly delusional.

How could he believe he would regain his parental authority over his son by killing Stephen's mother in cold blood? How could he believe he'd walk out of the shelter?

He had to know police had surrounded the place by now.

Delusional.

Ethan shivered. Mark's monologue gave him a pretty good idea where the man's state of mind was.

Mark was caught in a trap of his own making, and he knew it. He was probably open to making more mistakes, but that also meant a more volatile situation all around.

Any word, any movement, could set Mark off with fatal results.

Sweat pouring down his face, Mark finally looked at Ethan, and Ethan knew, as he made eye contact with the man, that this was the moment he'd been looking for.

Mark had turned the gun on him.

"If you want Stephen..." he said slowly, and then accelerated "...you're gonna have to go through me."

Ethan screamed like a banshee and plowed straight for the man with the gun with all the strength of his being.

Time slammed to a halt.

Mark let go of Lena and propped the gun with both hands, aiming straight at Ethan. But that didn't matter now. Ethan was beyond caring.

Glory pulled Lena away.

The women moved out of Ethan's peripheral vision.

Mark's, too, he thought.

The women were safe.

Something exploded.

Ethan thought the police must be closing in.

Still, he ran.

He must get to Mark. Must save everyone.

Glory yelled, "Bruno, come."

Bruno flew in from nowhere. A flash of fur.

Glory yelled again. "Bruno, *bite!*"

Ethan was confused. Off balance, as if in a dream.

He lunged for Mark, but Bruno beat him to the punch, wrestling the pistol away from the man.

Without a gun, the stakes were even, and Ethan tackled Mark and knocked him out cold. Even then, Ethan sat slumped over the man, pinning him down in case he regained consciousness.

He was taking no chances.

Lena was screaming wildly. Something about blood.

Blood. He was pretty sure he'd broken Mark's nose. There was blood.

Glory clucked around like a mother hen, directing people here and there. Counselors. Policemen. Someone called for an ambulance.

The mist fading, he was suddenly aware of a glaring pain in his left shoulder. He looked down.

Blood. More blood than on his knuckles.

For a moment he just looked.

Then he yelled, "Glory! I...think...need...sit... down."

Glory's face was pale. Worried. She looked like she might cry.

Ethan scowled, trying to think. Glory cry?

He gave her what he hoped was a smile, though it felt more like a grimace.

Suddenly he could no longer stand. He dropped to his knees.

"Gorgeous," he said with a coarse chuckle, "I think...that nozzle...shot me."

Chapter Sixteen

Glory paced across the room and back for the hundredth time. The doctor said Ethan was only sleeping, but he didn't so much as twitch in his sleep. She thought the effects of having his shoulder patched up was catching up with him.

At least the doctors said no permanent damage had been done. Still, she'd hated being away from him, even to tend to shelter details.

The first few hours after Mark had first entered the shelter, and then had shot Ethan had been a terrifying rush of activity, accompanied by a stomach-turning rush of adrenaline.

Mark himself had to be dealt with as a first order of business. Bruno had taken good care of the gun, and Ethan had knocked the man clean out, so the police had no trouble hauling him off.

Between what he'd done to Lena and shooting Ethan, he was looking at some serious jail time.

There would be more than enough time for Lena and her children to move on with their lives.

Lena had already taken her children and moved into a new shelter somewhere in western Washington, but Glory didn't think she'd be there for long.

Oddly enough, facing Mark off the way she had, hadn't sent Lena back into her shell; instead, she was more determined than ever to make a new life for herself and her children, far and away from the influence of Mark.

Bruno was heartily welcomed into the Angel's Wings family, by the mothers as much as the children. They were already begging Ginger to discuss with Glory the possibility of the addition of another dog to their troupe.

Mrs. Bruno? Glory's lip twitched upward. She'd bear it in mind.

All this had happened in such a short time, and Ethan still slept peacefully and oblivious in his hospital bed.

To say she was anxious to get the old Ethan back would be an understatement. When the gun went off in the hallway, for one moment Glory had realized the possibility of losing him.

Not only as a friend, someone she worked with at the shelter, but as someone who could take a cloudy day and make it bright. Someone who could make her laugh when she was down, and fly on his fancy just by his words.

She sat down at the chair by his bedside, wondering, as she had many times that day, why they made hospital chairs so uncomfortable.

Hers was a big, vinyl armchair thing that she couldn't get pushed close to the side of the bed, but that popped up an annoying footrest whenever she leaned backward.

One of the many paradoxes of life, she supposed.

Settled, she reached out tentatively and began stroking Ethan's silky blond hair. She loved the feel of his hair. Someone had washed it free of the blood that had dried there.

How would he take it, she wondered, her sudden change of heart. Or would he have known it all along, and it was only her stubborn heart that needed to learn how to yield.

Stubborn? Like *he* could talk about stubborn?

Running into a gun, for pity's sake. What kind of sense did that make? And yet, at the very same time, it was the greatest sort of bravery, to run headlong into danger for the sake of your ideals and the people you loved.

"You've paid your penance, you big oaf," she said aloud, kissing him lightly on the forehead where her fingers had just been. "You ran right into the wrong end of a gun. How smart is that, Wheeler?"

He didn't answer, of course. His breathing pattern hadn't changed. She chuckled.

"You're a hero. I've brought a newspaper for you to read when you feel like it. You didn't make the front page, but page two isn't bad for a first-time champion. Big, close up shot of your ugly mug and everything."

She took his hand, the one that wasn't attached to an IV, and began a long, stroking massage she'd learned in a class once. She hadn't had much use for it, since she lived alone.

But now...now there was Ethan.

Her heart swelled until she thought it might burst. The man of the hour, and he wanted her.

She'd asked herself why, and then again, why she would ever have wanted to throw away what she shared with Ethan. But for every answer, there were a thousand more questions.

For one, did he still want her?

"You know, it galls me to have to say you were right," she whispered, softly stroking his hand. "I don't do apologies well. But when I saw you on the other side of that gun...."

She chuckled and held up a hand. "Okay. Okay. You don't have to say anything. I'm an idiot."

Brushing a tear away, she leaned as far forward as she could, given the chair and the handrails on the bed, and placed her head on his chest, listened to the beat of his heart.

"When you're right, you're right. I do need you and Meggie in my life. You do make me a better person, and better able to help others. And I think I do the same for you."

Suddenly Ethan's arm slipped around her, and she jumped, but she stilled when she felt the chuckle in his ribs.

He brushed the hair away from her face with his hand. "Tell me," he said, pursing his lips in that half smirk, "Was that a proposal?"

"Ethan Wheeler, how long have you been eavesdropping on me?"

Of course, he ignored her question. "Because if it *was* a proposal, I accept."

"What?" she screeched, jumping away from him. The man was crazy. Certifiably crazy.

He just smiled contentedly. "When should we get married?"

"Married? Ethan, I'm still trying to figure out if you're lucid."

"Glory, hon, come back on over here." He patted the mattress beside him.

She sat daintily to avoid hurting him.

"You aren't the only one who had a revelation last night, Glory. Try looking down the barrel of a gun."

He looked away for a moment, but when he looked back, his gaze was clear and full of amusement. "I almost lost *me* last night, Glory," he said in a high-pitched squeak.

Glory chuckled. She just couldn't help it.

"I'm not leaving, Glory Weston. You can throw me out or run away, but I'm just going to keep coming back and chasing you."

She smiled. "I'm glad to hear it."

He narrowed his eyes on her. "Well?"

"Well?" She looked confused for a moment, and then blushed from her chin to the tip of her forehead.

Ethan grinned like a cat.

"I do."

He leaned on his good elbow and cocked his head. "You *do?*"

"I do."

"Well, then," he said, pursing his lips once again as if he had a secret to hide, "I guess the only question is, 'How do we do?'"

Ethan wanted to stretch his arms behind him and clasp his hands behind his neck, but that was kind of difficult to do in a sling. He was feeling great, really. He had wanted to go home since the first night he was there.

But the doctors had said *one more night, one more night* consistently, until the mimic of those words echoed in his head. Finally, though, three very long days and longer nights later, the doctors had given their go-ahead.

And with their go-ahead was his Go For It!

He'd just made the call—to Ginger Weston, his partner in crime.

"Is everything ready?" he asked anxiously as Ginger walked into his hospital room laden with bags.

She barked a laugh and set her arms akimbo on her hips. "Since when did you care if everything was ready? To hear Glory tell it, you'd be classified as more of a free spirit."

Ethan rolled with laughter, which hurt his

shoulder. Which, in turn, of course made him roll even harder with laughter.

"That's more like it," Ginger replied, tongue-in-cheek. "Now. I brought you everything you asked me to get, but I'm telling you right now, this is pushing too hard, too fast. Glory is never going to go for what you have planned."

Ethan just grinned and shrugged. "Maybe. Maybe not. Is my big brother here?"

"If you mean that good-looking, Stetson-toting, duster-wearing cowboy brooding in the waiting room, that would be him."

"Yeah," he agreed. "That would be him." His younger brother Rhett couldn't make it on such short notice, but Erik went out of his way, despite his surly exterior.

When everyone save Glory was present, they set their trap, putting it together piece by piece until it was perfectly assembled. Now all they— *he*—had to do was wait.

Wait. And sit and wonder if he was making yet another life-threatening mistake, just as potent and dangerous as running headlong into a bullet.

Maybe he could call it all off, on account of his shoulder hurting. Make it another day. They'd all understand.

And then the wait was over, and it was too late. For better or for worse, he was committed.

"Places everyone," Ginger pealed gaily.

Lights, camera and Hawaiian music.

"What is all this?" Glory asked the moment she entered his room. "Your music is loud enough to be heard down the hall. Don't you think you should be...."

Her sentence faded to nothing as, Ethan presumed, she suddenly became aware of her surroundings.

He held his breath, waiting to see if she'd play the nurse and have all these people gone. Waiting to see if she'd ban the party.

After all, she was in the middle of a luau.

It took her a moment. She gave everyone and everything a good hard look, from his cowboy of a brother to the red, fruity punch bowl covered with pineapple slices. The radio was blaring too loud. There were way too many people in the small room. She was certain there were health codes.

She crossed her arms as she turned to Ethan, and his heart nearly stopped cold. She didn't like his idea.

No, of course she didn't. She wouldn't.

What had he been doing, testing her? He

opened his mouth to apologize, but never made it that far.

"You were having a party without me?" Then she whirled and she whooped and she blew Ethan a kiss.

"Believe me, honey," Ginger said, "this is one party that *can't* start without you."

"I've got a shirt for you, gorgeous," Ethan said, reaching his gift to her. "It's my second-best shirt—I'm wearing the best one."

He chuckled, then coughed and stopped for a moment. "I'd have bought you a new one, but I couldn't get out on time."

Glory brought the shirt to her face and inhaled deeply of Ethan's brisk scent. "Believe me, this is better than new."

As she threw the shirt on over her sweater, Ginger presented her with a lei. "Congratulations, sis," she said formally, with a tear in her eye.

Glory's throat caught. "If you're getting mushy, something bigger than a party is going on here."

Ginger's eyes twinkled. "I'll give you a hint. That deliciously good-looking cowboy over there who is bouncing Meggie on his knees is Ethan's older brother, Erik."

"His brother?" Glory's eyes widened. "Excuse me while I have a quick little rendezvous with Ethan.''

Now that she noticed it, nearly everyone she worked with at the shelter was here, in addition to Ginger and Erik. The tone was clear enough.

Her panic instinct, that fight or flight, was setting off bells all over the place.

Sure, she wanted to marry Ethan. They'd sort of alluded to it the day after he'd been shot, and had talked quietly of their future together in the two days since.

But get married? In a hospital?

Wouldn't it be better to wait until he was healed, at the very least? Until they'd had more time to work on their relationship?

And then the picture of Ethan, Meggie and Bruno filling her tiny town house with warmth and love intruded, and she decided to play firefighter another day.

''Yes,'' she told Ethan as she approached. ''I mean, I do.''

''I do, too,'' he whispered huskily, leaning into her kiss for a moment. ''But I've paid a lot for the band. Can we say it before the minister, already? I can't wait to be married to you.''

''Your wish is my command,'' she said with a rolling bow.

Then, with a sly grin, she turned to the company and gave a sharp, two-fingered whistle. "Ginger and Meggie with me. Erik Wheeler, front and center. You're on."

She looked around, unable to account for one member of their party. "Has anyone seen the minister?"

"Present and accounted for," cried a small, bespectacled man standing up by Ethan's bed.

She took a second look when she realized the man was dressed in a flowery Hawaiian shirt over his clerical collar.

Ethan's doing. Would a lifetime be enough with that man?

She intended to find out.

* * * * *

Chapter One

"**Y**ou marry a man, not an occupation," Lakeisha Wilson said, loud and clear.

But it wasn't as if Julia Evans hadn't already considered every angle of her Great Scheme. It was simply a matter of helping Lakeisha grasp the concept.

"He is a man," Julia reasoned aloud. Smothering a smile, she coolly shifted her gaze to the subject in question—the Object of her Affection.

Well, not affection, precisely, but be that as it may...

Bryan Cummins.

Tall, dark and handsome.

More to the point, ordained.

He didn't know it yet, but she'd chosen him for a very special project.

Marriage.

Sunshine glistened off his straight, dark hair, and his smile was perfect and white. Practiced, even.

Father Bryan was surrounded by a raucous group of young men. Though he stood on the opposite side of the swimming pool from where Julia sat sipping her iced tea, she could tell he was in the middle of a heated theological discussion with his friends.

In Julia's experience with him, Bryan didn't speak about much else besides the tenets of the faith. His idea of polite conversation was debating the merits and nuances of each of the five points of Calvinism. With Scriptural proofs.

That, Julia supposed, was part of the allure. She glanced back to Lakeisha and chuckled merrily at the stunned look on her friend's face. She had obviously followed the direction of Julia's gaze and thoughts.

"I take it you don't approve of my Great Scheme."

Lakeisha snorted a laugh. "That's the understatement of the year."

Even as she shook her head disparagingly at

Julia, Lakeisha smiled pleasantly to a couple of working associates who'd stopped to say hello. Julia recognized the woman as being from the accounting office at HeartBeat, and cheerfully pointed them in the direction of the iced tea.

As she looked around, she realized nearly every employee of the HeartBeat Crisis Pregnancy Center was here for this late summer gathering at the Martins.

People crowded around the pool, though no one was swimming. A few wore swimsuits, but mostly Julia saw casual summer wear, and in some cases, well-coordinated and assuredly expensive matching outfits. Bryan fell into that category.

She leaned back in her chair and smiled. She didn't know many names, but the faces were familiar. There was Mr. Movie in his dark sunglasses and little else, and Merry Maid, who always picked up after everyone in the office. In the far corner was her boss, Sarah Straight-Arrow, speaking to Little Miss Muffet, who was forever on a persistent insect-killing mission. Julia squirmed at the thought, disliking spiders, herself.

Julia didn't mind the crowd; unlike Lakeisha, who preferred a good book to a raging party. But then, Lakeisha probably knew all the names and backgrounds that went with these people, instead of the safe but not very effective stereotypes Julia tended to slap on them.

"I'm not finished with you, girl," Lakeisha warned when they were alone once again. "Because I'm not getting the point of your little plan at all." She waved one hand and propped the other on her hip. "You've gone completely out of your mind, girl, and I'm not following."

"It's not like I'm picking a name out of a telephone book or putting my face on a billboard."

"Oh, no, of course not. Your system is so-o-o-o much better. Excuse me, sir. May I see your resume?" Her high, squeaky tone suggested her cynicism.

Julia laughed. "It isn't as coldhearted as all that. I simply feel that I'm ready to move to the next level, you know? I'm twenty-eight years old, and I don't even feel like a grown-up."

Lakeisha laughed. "And that's bad?"

"Depends on your perspective, I guess. Right now, marrying a decent, godly, professional man is a critical part of my equation. What could be wrong with that?"

As soon as the question was out, Julia regretted asking. It was like inviting a politician to share her views on the economy. Lakeisha Wilson, her dear friend of more than twenty-four years, would certainly want to expound on the many hazards and pitfalls of Julia's plan to choose her own husband.

And knowing Lakeisha, she'd enjoy every gruesome moment of it.

Right on cue, Lakeisha grinned like a cat and raised her eyebrows so high they were lost underneath her wiry black bangs. "Okay, first of all, what is wrong with this little scenario of yours is that you can't just choose a man at random, and then expect him to agree on the spot to marry you."

Lakeisha had a point there, Julia acknowledged. But it wasn't an insurmountable difficulty. She'd just get to know Bryan a little better.

Okay, a lot better. But it could be done.

"You think just because you made a decision that Bryan meets your marital requirements, that he is going to ask you to marry him?"

"Not right away, of course, but—"

"What about sparks and fireworks, Julia? Don't you want to fall in love?"

Julia shrugged. Sparks and fireworks were an overrated commodity, in her mind. She could live without them, and good riddance.

"Look around you. Right here in this backyard.

Look at all these young, eligible, handsome Christian men. Why settle for someone you don't even know? What if there's someone special out there, someone God made just for you?"

Julia raised an eyebrow. "Oh, right. Such as?"

"Well..." Lakeisha paused, just as a large shadow passed across them. Seeing the cause of the shadow, she smiled widely. "How about Zeke Taylor?"

"Paul Bunyon?" Julia spouted a laugh. "I always picture that man in the company of a big, snorting blue ox."

"Julia!"

"Well, I do."

Zeke Taylor was a local carpenter who volunteered his time to the shelter. Well over six feet tall, he was blonde, bearded, and always wore flannel shirts and steel-toed boots. A lumberjack wasn't such a big stretch.

"Zeke!" Lakeisha called, to Julia's immediate distress.

The big man turned and strode back to where they sat, then crouched beside them with a smile. Julia had to admit he had the biggest, bluest eyes she'd ever seen.

His kind, friendly gaze looked directly at her. She felt as if he were really seeing her, not merely giving her a polite perusal. She swallowed dryly and struggled to erase the imprint of his smile in her mind.

"What can I do for you ladies?" His voice was the low, rich bass she expected it to be. Julia had the uncomfortable notion the question was directed at her.

"Julia and I have just been discussing true love," Lakeisha began, despite Julia's stricken look in her direction. "We were wondering about your opinion on the topic."

Zeke laughed, and Julia was struck again by how genuinely friendly he appeared. "That's an awfully big topic."

Julia just barely restrained herself from saying that he was an awfully big man. But Lakeisha clearly captured her train of thought, and they shared an amused, meaning-filled glance.

"Let me narrow it down for you," Julia said, deciding it was better to take the bull by the horns, so to speak, than to sit there and let Lakeisha dictate the conversation. "Do you believe there is a Mr. Right?"

Zeke slapped his palm against his broad chest. "For me, I'd have to say no."

Lakeisha roared with laughter, and didn't stop even when Julia pinned her with a glare.

"That's not what I meant and you know it."

Zeke nodded, his amused glance sliding over Lakeisha and landing squarely on Julia. "I didn't believe it was. I was just joshing you."

Her eyes widened. "Oh."

He cleared his throat. "I know I sometimes come off gruff, because of my size..." He ground to a halt, and then continued tentatively. "People often mistake my meaning, too."

"You didn't answer the question," reminded Lakeisha, who continued to struggle composing her features. "Do you believe God has one special someone out there for you?"

"One special woman," Zeke said slowly, catching Julia's gaze with his own. "This is now bone of my bones, and flesh of my flesh... She's out there, Lord willing."

"Waiting for you?" Julia queried softly.

Zeke shook his head. "No. Not waiting for me." He ran a hand over his beard and smiled. "Working. Serving the Lord wherever she's at."

Julia tried to swallow and couldn't. Why did that sound so romantic, coming from a guy who wore a plain white T-shirt to a pool party, and whose biceps were probably larger around than the breadth of her waist?

"You'll excuse me," she said, her words tumbling one over another. "I need to go ask Father Bryan about something."

It was true—she did need to speak to Bryan about the upcoming ad campaign at HeartBeat. So why did her words feel so much like a lie?

She hurried away from Zeke and Lakeisha as fast as she could without looking rude, glancing back only once to see Zeke following her progress with his gaze. Flustered, she spoke to everyone she passed, trying to make up for what felt like rudeness by being extra kind to everyone she met.

When she reached Father Bryan, she laid an arm on his shoulder to get his attention, then waited quietly while he finished his conversation with some of his seminary buddies. She didn't understand half the words they were saying, and wondered if, as a pastor's wife, she'd have to get a seminary education herself, just to communicate with her husband.

Husband.

She glanced up at Bryan, picturing them together in her mind. Helping others, like the desperate, pregnant mothers who came into Heart-Beat. Like the people in his congregation, wherever God led. Who knew what else they could accomplish?

She waited, but there was nothing.

No quickening of her heartbeat, no chills, or flush, or loss of breath or—anything. Not a single emotion.

But marriage wasn't about emotion. Weddings might be, but she'd seen firsthand how quickly those feelings faded. Wasn't her way better?

"Julia?" Bryan looked a little put out, and she wondered if he'd tried more than once to get a hold of her wandering attention.

"I'm sorry. I was woolgathering."

"Not a problem. I should be the one apologizing for making you wait." He flashed her a toothy grin.

Julia wondered if that was what his true smile looked like.

"I just wanted to chat with you about the new ad campaign," Julia began, though Bryan's attention, or at least his gaze, was wandering elsewhere. "If now is a bad time…"

"Not at all." His gaze returned to her, and he smiled squarely. "I've assembled some Scripture passages we can use on the brochures, but I'm still working up something for the full-page magazine ad."

"That's fine, but we need a mock-up of the ad by Thursday noon at the latest."

His gaze shifted to somewhere over her left

shoulder. "I've got classes Monday and Wednesday, but I'll try to fit it in on Tues—what is that?"

"What is what?" Disheartened by her failure to capture Bryan's attention, never mind his interest, Julia spun around to see where he was looking.

It didn't take long to find the source of his surprise. A dirty, brown and white Jack Russell Terrier had somehow gotten through the high fence surrounding the backyard. She knew the Martins didn't own any animals, which would have been prohibitive for their ministry lifestyle.

At first it was amusing, watching the guests' varied reactions to the filthy animal, but it was another thing entirely to discover the poor thing was limping, favoring its left back foot. Julia wondered if he'd been hit by a car.

She decided she should take care of the dog, especially since no one else appeared to be moving. She wanted to contain him in case he was hurt or bleeding. Then she'd call a vet.

She turned to let Bryan know she was leaving, but his attention was elsewhere. He burst into laughter.

"Well, I'll be doggoned," he said, shaking his head. "What a crazy mutt."

She whirled around. To her surprise, the Jack

Russell had somehow launched itself into the swimming pool.

"What a joke," Bryan said from behind her.

A joke? Maybe, under normal circumstances. But within seconds, it was clear the dog could not swim. It flipped into the middle of the pool and disappeared under the waves.

Panic freezing her to the spot, she croaked Bryan's name.

But it wasn't Bryan who came running to the poor little dog's rescue.

It was big, burly Zeke Taylor. In a second, he was in the pool, pulling the dog to the surface and into his arms. He hadn't waited even to remove his steel-toed boots. He'd simply reacted. And saved the dog, who was wagging his tail in Zeke's arms despite being wet.

Bryan was still laughing at the sight. She guessed it was funny, from one perspective, but Julia could have no reaction except sheer admiration for Zeke Taylor's heroic effort.

Chapter Two

Glancing at the sky, Zeke Taylor stopped pounding nails into a two-by-four frame. Swiping in a deep breath of sawdust-filled air, he pulled out a crumpled red bandana from the back pocket of his faded blue jeans and mopped the sweat off his forehead.

Guessing from the position of the sun, it had to be at least ten o'clock, which meant that his assistant on this project, Dane Kennedy, was late. Again.

Other contractors and their laborers swarmed around the house, but Zeke had yet to see Dane Kennedy among them.

What did that make, now? Three times in four days?

Zeke knew he should fire the young man, but couldn't find it in his heart to do so. It certainly put him in an awkward position. Zeke was responsible for getting his work done, which he couldn't do without another set of hands.

And how would Dane learn the meaning of responsibility if not confronted by the issue?

Dane should be fired.

That was the high and low of it, and Zeke knew it. The young man was willing to stay as late as it took to get the job done, to make up for his perpetual tardiness. But that wasn't the point, was it?

Zeke scratched his beard, wondering what God would have him do. Zeke was a spiritual seed planter, and hoped to have the opportunity to share God's love with Dane. The young man wasn't offended with the mention of God, but he clearly wasn't impressed, either. He was the tried-and-true original, take-life-by-the-seat-of-the-pants kind of guy.

Zeke blew out a frustrated breath and picked up his hammer, hoping to find solace in punching nails. Or maybe he would concentrate on something more pleasant, like the silver-toned laugh of a certain gorgeous blond-haired, blue-eyed angel he could never fully get out of his mind.

Especially after yesterday.

He pounded five nails in a row, slamming them neatly into a row. His anger over Dane only helped his strength.

Even without the strong emotion, Zeke could punch nails with his hammer faster than a man with a nail gun. More accurate, too, he thought, though he'd never tested his theory.

"Hard day?" asked a laughing tenor voice from behind him.

"It's ten o'clock, Dane." Zeke whirled around, his voice deepening in anger. "Work here starts at seven a.m. sharp."

He almost added *young man*, but consciously stopped himself short, realizing Dane would take offense.

Even knowing that angered Zeke. It wasn't Dane's fault he felt like a father in the first place, even if there was only a twelve-year difference in their ages.

Dane only grinned like a schoolboy. "Yeah, I know. Overslept my alarm. I think my cat must have hit it or something." He ruffled his hand through his thick, red-blond hair and belted an uneven laugh.

"You don't have a cat," Zeke reminded him, tightening the grip on his hammer.

Dane dropped his gaze to the floor. "I know. My record isn't real clean. I'm surprised you haven't fired me already."

Zeke chuckled low in his chest. "I'm surprised I haven't fired you already. I'm trusting God on this one, Dane. But this is your last shot."

"Not very rational," Dane mumble under his breath as he picked up his tool belt and strapped it on with some difficulty.

"Trying to talk yourself out of a job?"

"No," he protested immediately with a wave of his hand. "But let me make it up to you. Take you out for a beer or something after work."

Zeke lifted a brow.

"Ah, I should have known you wouldn't go for a beer."

He chuckled. "That's hardly the point, now, is it? What bar lets an underage boy inside to drink beer?" Then he shook his head. "No. Don't answer that. I don't want to know."

"We can get a soda or something," Dane inserted, avoiding the question even as he wrinkled his nose in distaste at the thought of the tamer liquid. "Do you play pool?"

"Yes, but I can't tonight."

"It's okay," Dane snapped, stalking away.

"Dane." Zeke's booming voice echoed through the job site.

Dane turned, scowling. "Give me a rain check on pool, will you? I'm volunteering down at HeartBeat tonight."

Dane looked relieved, but still couldn't help himself not to make another wisecrack. "The pregnancy center. Excitement personified."

"Knock it off with the attitude, buddy," Zeke snapped, losing all patience with the young man. It was one thing for the boy to make fun of everything else in and around Zeke's life, but it was quite another to disparage HeartBeat, an organization that truly helped women and their unborn babies—helped them eat, find shelter and prepare for childbirth.

To his surprise, Dane burst into laughter.

"What is your problem?" Zeke was a patient man, but at the moment, Dane was very close to losing his job permanently.

"There's a woman involved. You're going to see a woman tonight."

Zeke's breath left his lungs as if someone sucker punched him. "Excuse me?" he croaked.

"I've never seen you get so riled up about anything. Who is she? What's her name?"

Zeke went back to pounding nails, desperately

hoping Dane would just drop the subject. It was one of the many things he admired most about Julia—how devoted she was to the Center. She worked days and many evenings, not to mention weekends, helping other people personally as well as being in charge of the Center's advertising.

But how could he clarify to Dane that Julia was usually at the Center, but that she wasn't the reason he volunteered?

He prayed that was the truth.

It had to be.

Dane wouldn't drop the subject without a fight. "Come on, Zeke, just give me a name. It'll help me remember you're human. Main man Zeke with his lady friend."

Zeke shook his head and mumbled, "Julia."

"What?"

"Julia, okay?" he said louder. "And she's not my lady friend."

"Just Julia. She'll be there at the center tonight, right, cuz?"

"Yeah, she'll be there." He hoped.

Dane pounded him on the back, then left him alone with his thoughts and moved to the other side of the building.

Zeke wasn't sure he wanted to be alone with his dark, ugly thoughts roaring up to haunt him.

When had his motivation for helping out at the clinic become because Julia Evans was there?

Was it true?

She'd only just spoken to him for the first time yesterday at the pool party, and even then it was because of her friend Lakeisha. And yet he had to admit that the desire to see her again ranked right up there with the desire to do good works.

His thoughts tearing him up, he worked frantically, until suddenly he heard her voice.

"Zeke? Zeke Taylor?"

Now he was hallucinating. Next he'd be put in a straightjacket. He whistled a birdsong and imagined stars floating over his head.

"Hello! May I come up there?"

Zeke turned around to see none other than the true-to-the-flesh Julia Evans slip-sliding her way down a steep, gravel-covered driveway and onto the job site. Her arms flapped wildly as she struggled to maintain her precarious balance.

She wasn't dressed for visiting a construction job site. For one thing, she was wearing a dress. A pretty, soft, satiny looking thing that Zeke might make disintegrate underneath his rough fingertips. And heels. High heels from the looks of them, sinking into the gravel with every step.

Feeling like a lumbering giant, he trotted to her

side and offered his arm for assistance. Her eyes widened to enormous proportions as she laid her hand upon his forearm and allowed his other arm to encircle her tiny waist, and Zeke wished for the millionth time that he wasn't so big. Sure, men admired his strength, but to a delicate woman like Julia, he knew he must come off as a big, dumb ox.

For Julia's part, her lungs had simply refused to work from the moment Zeke jogged to her side to the time she stood safely at the top of the hill. He was so athletic, muscles and ligaments working in perfect harmony. His autumn-blond hair shone like gold.

Only she couldn't even enjoy the picture, for she was about to plunge head-down the gravel driveway. Her shoes were the worst possible choice, and she was embarrassed that she hadn't given her attire a thought when she came here.

What must Zeke think of her? He was all kindness, offering his brawny arm so she could push and twist her way up the hill. But honestly, what kind of an idiot wore patent leather pumps to a construction site?

Even Zeke had a hard hat on.

As if seeing the direction of her gaze, Zeke moved to a trunk and picked up an extra hard hat.

"I'm afraid I'm going to have to..." He cleared his throat. "...ask you to wear one of these for the length of your visit. It's for your own safety, as well as our regulations." He tacked the last part on so swiftly that Julia could barely understand the words.

She thought she saw Zeke cringe slightly, as if anticipating her answer. He no doubt thought, based on the little he knew of her, that she'd criticize or whine.

Well, she'd do neither, she thought, reaching for the hard hat with her best smile. Even though she knew she'd look ridiculous. Even though the hat was two sizes too big.

Zeke jammed his big paws into his front jeans pockets and raised his eyebrows. His huge blue eyes were gleaming with mischief, and she was certain she could see the corner of his mouth twitch under his beard.

Her dander rose quickly, and just as quickly departed. "Feel free to laugh out loud," she said wryly, and with a smile.

A bubble of deep, hearty laughter burst out, though he looked like he was struggling desperately to restrain it.

"Sorry," he apologized when he could speak. He wiped his eyes with his thumb. "It's just that you're the cutest carpenter I've ever seen on a job site.''

She curtsied slightly. ''I'll take that as a compliment, thank you very much.''

There was an extended silence where Zeke collected his mirth and Julia collected her thoughts.

''Did you come here about HeartBeat?'' he asked quietly, leaning against the framework he'd earlier been pounding upon.

''Not directly, no.'' Julia's heart began to race.

Yesterday, at the pool party, Zeke had left as soon as he'd gotten the dog from the pool, an act she still considered tremendously heroic.

What measure of a man jumped into the pool with his boots on to save an animal?

''Actually, I came to find out about that little Jack Russell Terrier you rescued. Is he okay?''

''Tip? Yeah, *she's* fine.'' He cocked his head and stood silently for a moment, taking in her mettle. ''You really care?''

''I think I proved my worth with my pumps.'' When he looked stumped, she continued. ''My high heels.''

He grinned. ''You have a point.''

''How do you know her name is Tip?'' she asked, self-consciously fiddling with her hard hat.

"Because I named her. Do you want to see her?"

"She's here?" Julia asked in astonishment. "At the construction site?"

He nodded. "I didn't want to leave her alone all day."

Julia's heart fell. "Is she hurt bad, then?"

Offering his hand, Zeke shook his head. "Her leg is broken. And I think there's a screw loose in that brain of hers, jumping into the pool the way she did."

"Oh, no," Julia objected. "I'm sure she thought she could swim."

Zeke chuckled. "Yeah. Thought being the key word. Seriously, though, she's going to be just fine. Nothing a little R&R can't fix."

One step at a time, he led her back up the gravel to where his truck was parked. In the bed of his truck, tucked securely into a torn box and curled up on an old scrap of blanket, was Tip.

Zeke picked her up, and she immediately wagged her tail and began licking his chin.

"You can sure tell who Tip likes," Julia teased. "It didn't take you two long to form an attachment."

Color crept up Zeke's cheeks above his beard, and Julia smiled in delight. There was nothing made up about Zeke Taylor. He was all man, and completely genuine.

"She didn't have a home, so I gave her one," Zeke explained tenderly. As he spoke, he petted the dog mechanically. Julia marveled at how gentle Zeke's big hands looked on the small dog.

"So she'll recover completely?" Julia reached forward to stroke the dog's wiry coat. Tip had had a bath, she noticed.

"Completely. And she has a home. She can keep me company, and I can keep her away from large bodies of water."

They laughed pleasantly together.

"I bought some things for the dog," Julia stated softly.

"Things?"

"Bowls for food and water. A collar and leash. A couple of squeaky toys. Dog bones. And a big bag of dog food. That's all," she concluded, feeling suddenly foolish for coming out to the site.

Zeke had things well in hand, and he didn't need her interference. Of course he never made her feel that way, but it was obvious she wasn't needed here.

She hadn't even been sure she could find Tip again, and yet she'd felt compelled to visit the local pet store. Buying things for the dog was a kind of catharsis, she supposed; a way of doing something now, when inertia had kept her from helping yesterday at the pool.

The longer Julia's list grew the wider Zeke's gaze grew.

"What?" Julia asked, wondering if he were going to call her an idiot. She would call her an idiot. What a dumb thing to do.

She could have at least called first and asked if he needed anything.

But she was always going off half-cocked, trying to help when she was really just in the way. Perhaps she'd learn her lesson this time.

"You are a godsend," Zeke said, carefully replacing Tip in her box.

Julia felt like someone had brushed a finger down her spine. Adrenaline coursed through her. "What?"

He turned to her, leaning his muscular arm against the side of his truck. His eyes gleamed with a combination of appreciation and genuine admiration that made Julia's stomach swirl with unusual and unnamable emotions.

Zeke continued, his voice low and resolute. "Unfortunately, I barely made it to the vet's yesterday afternoon, and then Tip needed looking after. I haven't gotten anything for her. I've been feeding her with the sample food the vet gave me.''

"You don't have anything?" she repeated numbly.

"Anything. Or is that nothing?" He smiled widely and belted a laugh. "So you see, Julia, you're an answer to a prayer today. A blessing disguised as an angel."

This time, it was Julia's turn to blush.

Chapter Three

Julia thought about Zeke all the way back to the apartment she shared with Lakeisha. She was surprised to find Zeke was a lot like her in many ways. Who, for example, would rescue a dog and then keep it?

She realized with a start she should be thinking about Bryan. It was just as well, for thinking about him didn't confuse her or make her feel funny—happy and sad at the same time. Or threatened and safe.

Give her security any day of the week. And Father Bryan was security. She resolved once more to pursue her plans with Bryan as she pushed the key in the doorknob.

The scene that met her eyes reminded her of a detective novel she'd once read. Sofa cushions were overthrown, the newspaper tossed in random segments down the hall, and the pictures on the wall sat askew.

Her first impression was that a thief had mercilessly ransacked the apartment. She resisted the urge to flee the room and call 911.

Instead, she entered the living room more fully for a closer inspection. Upon further observance, she decided it looked more the work of a natural disaster than a clumsy thief.

And her suspicions rose. "Lakeisha? Are you home?"

No answer.

The wastebasket next to the desk had been knocked over and the contents scattered. In contrast, the contents of the desk drawers had remained undisturbed.

Definitely not the work of a burglar.

So what was it?

A tornado that hit only inside her apartment?

A scavenger or wild animal trapped inside here somewhere?

She considered and discarded one preposterous idea after another.

But the truth?

She hadn't a clue.

She tossed her purse down on the kitchen counter and headed for the bedroom to change. Lakeisha's bed was rumpled, her plain green-plaid bedspread crumpled in a heap. That in itself was a surprise.

But even more so was Lakeisha herself, who was slouched in her white wicker chair, looking as if she were in shock. Her glazed-over look and the state of their apartment would have scared Julia if it weren't for her friend's normal breathing and the sickly-sweet smile that told her Lakeisha was somewhere in La-La Land.

"Do you need a doctor?" Julia asked abruptly, just to test her friend's reaction, and shake her up a bit. "Should I call 911?"

"What? No!" Lakeisha snapped out of her reverie, bolting straight up in a moment and staring back at Julia as if she were crazy. Lakeisha's black eyes, flecked with gold and dancing with delight, told a story Julia definitely wanted to hear.

Julia lifted an eyebrow. "No? You're sure? I've got the phone right here." She waved the portable telephone under Lakeisha's nose.

She laughed, honey-rich and low. "No, girl, whatever else I may need, I don't need a doctor."

"Merry Maids, then?" Julia asked wryly.

"I know. It's weird. I'll clean up the house. Cross my heart. But Julia...I found him!"

"Who?" asked Julia, as perplexed by her friend's behavior as she was by the state of her residence. "The guy who trashed our apartment?"

Lakeisha giggled.

Giggled!

"I'm the guilty party. I was just so excited that I got a little carried away celebrating."

"I can see that," Julia said, looking around her pointedly. Then the second half of Lakeisha's statement penetrated her mind and she put her arms akimbo and narrowed her gaze on her very odd-acting friend. "Celebrating what?"

"Not what. Who. The guy."

"What guy, Lakeisha?" Julia snapped, thoroughly confused.

Hugging herself with her arms, Lakeisha looked at her friend and smiled whimsically.

"Mr. Right."

"I've got the perfect idea!" Julia exclaimed, bouncing out of her chair. "If Steven is too uncomfortable meeting me one-on-one, we could get a bunch of people together for a dinner party."

Julia had coaxed Lakeisha out of the bedroom and had finally gotten some semblance of a story from her. Lakeisha had been in an elevator going up to see her dentist on the eleventh floor, when suddenly, at the sixth floor, he had walked in. Steven Carver.

And somehow, between floors six and eleven, Lakeisha had fallen head-over-ears in love with the man. Julia was suspicious and, though she admitted it only to herself, more than a little jealous, for Steven appeared to return Lakeisha's sentiment.

Now the two women sat facing one another across their kitchen table, a country oak that was a firm compromise between the two ladies' taste in decor.

"He's more afraid of meeting you than my parents." Lakeisha laughed. "He's expecting Atilla the Hun, I think. I told him that you had to approve of the men I go out with. And that you aren't easy to please."

"What's a friend for, if not that," Julia observed, the corners of her mouth turning up. She held up her hand like a witness on the stand. "I do solemnly swear to do my duty as your best friend in the matter of judging Steven fit to be taking you out."

She grinned widely and waggled her eyebrows. "And I promise I won't bite—hard."

"Did I mention he's in the military?"

"Only about a hundred times." Julia shook her head. How someone could go over and over a person's physical attributes, she would never know.

"Well, don't worry," Lakeisha replied, as if reading her mind. "You'll understand someday, when you have a love of your own."

"I don't plan to have a love of my own," Julia reminded blandly.

Lakeisha's black eyes gleamed. "I wouldn't be too sure about that. In any case, let's do this dinner thing. Who should we invite?"

Julia rummaged through a drawer for a pad of paper and a pen. "How about Steven?"

Lakeisha giggled.

Julia hoped it would get better. Fast.

"I don't want it to be a big party, and scare Steven off."

"Well, we wouldn't want that, would we," Julia agreed dryly. "Let's just invite—"

"Bryan," Lakeisha finished for her.

"Are you feeling generous? I didn't think you approved of Bryan."

"It's not that I don't approve of Bryan, Julia,"

Lakeisha explained. "I just don't think he's the right man for you."

"He is," Julia muttered, cupping her chin in her palms. "He just doesn't know it yet."

"Well, I'm sure you'll take care of that soon enough," Lakeisha confirmed, with only the slightest hint of sarcasm lacing her voice. "Now, who else?"

"Zeke Taylor," Julia blurted, and then wanted to crawl under the table.

Lakeisha raised a brow. "Girlfriend, you never cease to amaze me."

"Why? Because it occurred to me to invite a nice Christian man who is obviously on his own to a full-course dinner which he probably doesn't get very often?"

"Not at all," replied Lakeisha with a laugh. "Because he's one good-looking hunk of man."

It was a busy night for HeartBeat. Their annual advertising blitz was scheduled for August, where various staff members would make speeches at churches and where volunteers would go door-to-door handing out literature to interested parties. There were so many needs in Denver, so much work HeartBeat had to do, not only in taking care of pregnant women and their babies, but in connecting with them in the first place.

And that was the theme of this year's campaign:

Get the Word Out.

Tonight alone, there were groups of volunteers folding brochures and doing mailings. Others were working out a campaign strategy on a big map pinned on a prominent wall. Phones were ringing off the hook, and there weren't enough people to answer them. Zeke even saw the building's janitor on duty, mopping his way around the compound.

The only person he didn't see was Julia, and he was dismayed to find it mattered very much to him that she wasn't there.

Oh, he was working, hammering together frames that would back some of the major signs. But his busy hands didn't take away the dead stillness of his heart.

"There are bound to be some dry times," Julia muttered to herself, closing her Bible with an audible thump.

Maybe it was just that she was reading through the Minor Prophets. Maybe it was just that she was distracted.

Zeke the Carpenter and Tip the Wonder Dog. Lakeisha finding Mr. Right.

Well, stranger things had happened.

Julia remembered with longing the times when she just couldn't get enough of God's Word. Now it seemed she had to struggle through each and every paragraph.

"Lord, what am I doing wrong?" she whispered in misery.

Julia walked outside onto the small balcony of her apartment and leaned as far into the redwood railing to see around the corner of the building. The wood had eroded from the elements and she had to be careful for slivers, but it was worth the discomfort.

Besides, it had been her habit since childhood to watch the sun rise. She breathed deeply, letting all her stress go for that one moment. The warmth on her face was like an instant connection with the Son. In His arms was true warmth.

It was her favorite time of the morning, where the world was still fresh and clean, and not marred by the contents of the day. As always, she wondered what this day would bring. Only God knew.

Lakeisha was a late sleeper, so early morning was Julia's special time with the Lord. Armed with her Bible and a stout cup of cocoa, she'd perched on the edge of her antique Victorian rocking chair and met with God.

And it was a good thing, too, because she sometimes talked aloud when she prayed. Like this morning.

"I'm not doing enough, am I?" she asked, looking up at the cloudy sky as if waiting for an audible answer, though of course she knew better than that. Oh, that life were so easy.

As she looked back down at her worn leather Bible, she traced the gold lettering that graced the front. As much as she'd like her answers face-to-face, she settled for knowing she could take Bible 101 when she got to heaven and have all her questions answered to her satisfaction.

The telephone rang, and she raced to the kitchen to grab the phone off the wall. She juggled and then dropped the receiver in her haste to answer before the ringing disturbed Lakeisha.

Swiping up the receiver from where it dangled near her feet, she cleared her throat, muttered a greeting, and once again dropped the receiver on the floor.

She stared down at it, praying desperately for a way out of this situation, for on the other end of the line was the one man's voice she *never* wanted to hear again, not ever.

So help her God.

Dear Reader,

I don't know about you, but I've been in Glory Weston's shoes a time or two. I fight the good fight, surround myself with what I believe is God's work and I strive to fulfill His will with all my might.

And sometimes, like Glory, I'm suddenly surprised to realize I can't see the forest for the trees.

I want to do what is right. I strive for what is good. But sometimes, in my zeal, I set up a target, pursue a goal or make a way for myself that isn't God's best for me, however good and right it may be in itself.

Today, open your eyes and watch for God's special blessings to arrive in your life. I'm praying He'll surprise you even today with His goodness, in ways you yourself never envisioned!

I love hearing from my readers, and would love to know what you thought of Ethan and Glory's story. I'm at P.O. Box 9806, Denver CO, 80209.

Surprises and Blessings in the LORD!

Deb Kastner

Next month
from Steeple Hill's

Love Inspired®

HEAVEN SENT
by
Jillian Hart

*Successful photographer Hope Ashton comes home to
Montana to care for her grandmother and encounters old
flame Matthew Shaw, a widower raising triplet sons. Soon
Matthew's mother and Hope's grandmother are hatching a
plan to bring them together. With lives as different as day
and night, will they discover that their love for God and
each other can bring them together?*

**Don't miss
HEAVEN SENT
On sale July 2001**

Love Inspired®

Visit us at www.steeplehill.com

LIHS